Living 'down Kent' over the shop his parents had bought had sounded great to Paul when he first heard about it. But Cherry Tree Estate turned out to be just rows and rows of grey houses at the end of a bus route. There was nowhere to go and nothing to do, but things would be better once he went to school, Paul told himself, especially if he could get into the school football team. That would be a ready-made set-up for him : a bit of friendship, the chance to show what he could do with a ball and, best of all, a sense of belonging somewhere again. It would be great to hear the rallying cry, 'All my men!' in the playground and know that it included him.

But getting into the team wasn't such a simple matter, after all. To make sure of being chosen, a player had to be in the good books of the toughest, most domineering boy in the school, Billy Richardson, and the price he demanded for accepting Paul into his clique involved favours Paul wasn't sure he wanted to pay. Desperate to start feeling at home in the strange, sometimes hostile world of his new school, and not to have to stay on its fringe with unpopular boys like Arthur, Paul found himself drifting further and further under Billy's control. It was only with time that he began to think there might be ways of 'belonging' that wouldn't mean losing his self-respect. Perhaps he didn't always have to be a follower – perhaps there were some situations in which *he* could take charge.

Bernard Ashley has set down the tensions of having to adapt to strange surroundings, and the excitement of learning from new experience, with the sensitive and honest realism which is his special quality.

Bernard Ashley was born in Woolwich, South London, in 1935 and educated at Blackheath and Rochester. After National Service in the RAF, he trained as a teacher and is now head master of a large multi-racial school. He is married to a teacher and has three sons. He lives in Charlton, not far from the scenes of his early childhood.

BREAK IN THE SUN

DINNER LADIES DON'T COUNT

DODGEM

HIGH PAVEMENT BLUES

I'M TRYING TO TELL YOU

JANEY

A KIND OF WILD JUSTICE

RUNNING SCARED

TERRY ON THE FENCE

THE TROUBLE WITH DONOVAN CROFT

ALL MY MEN

*

BERNARD ASHLEY

PUFFIN BOOKS

PUFFIN BOOKS

Published by the Penguin Group
Penguin Books Ltd, 27 Wrights Lane, London W8 5TZ, England
Penguin Books USA Inc., 375 Hudson Street, New York, New York 10014, USA
Penguin Books Australia Ltd, Ringwood, Victoria, Australia
Penguin Books Canada Ltd, 10 Alcorn Avenue, Toronto, Ontario, Canada M4V 3B2
Penguin Books (NZ) Ltd, 182–190 Wairau Road, Auckland 10, New Zealand

Penguin Books Ltd, Registered Offices: Harmondsworth, Middlesex, England

First published by Oxford University Press 1977
Published in Puffin Books 1979
7 9 10 8

Printed in England by Clays Ltd, St Ives plc
Set in Intertype Baskerville

Chapter One

THERE came a time, after you'd stayed in bed for so long in the morning, when your conscience forced you out of the hot groove your body had made and into your clothes. The sheets seemed to lose their luxury and you found yourself wriggling to avoid the wrinkles under your backside, searching for fresh cool places for your feet. Too much of a good thing, it seemed, turned on you in the end.

It was getting on for eleven o'clock when Paul Daines was forced to give up. For the past hour he'd been aware of the constant ding of the shop bell beneath him, the clatter of the closing door, and the murmur of voices; now, uncomfortable, and upset at the thought of his mum and dad being run off their feet downstairs, he pulled on his clothes and put a dampish flannel, still hard at the edges, round his face. Not that lying-in had been his choice that Sunday. He'd offered to help, serving from the freezer, or stacking empties, or packing the groceries in boxes; but he was too young yet, they'd said; he'd get under their feet and make mistakes with the change; and besides, grown-ups didn't like to be served by children. So he wasn't required. Well, they were dead wrong. He could be useful. The family stalls down in the market proved that. Down there even the nippers tore the tissue paper off the fruit, kept the racks full and shouted the odds. 'Who wants oranges? Four for ten p!' But they were new to business, the Daineses; they'd only had the shop a fortnight, and up to now they'd wanted to do it all themselves, to account personally for every ha'penny.

Perhaps it wasn't all that surprising, though. When

you've never had much money and a windfall comes your way you have to take good care of it. You have to be sure. Especially when it means the chance to do what his dad had done and give up the job you hate to be your own boss.

Paul was suddenly aware of the loudness of his sigh. The trouble was there was nowhere to go, nothing to do, and no one to do it with. He didn't start at the new school till the next morning so he had no mates yet; and this estate was a dead-and-alive hole, rows and rows of grey corrugated-roofed houses, a pub or two, a school, and the little parade of shops where they were now. It was the end of the bus route, stuck out on the edge of Eastfleet – 'Cherry Tree Estate' – and it had as much in common with the place they'd come from in London as a bleak puddle had with a colourful fish tank. The school looked flat, prefabricated and windswept, and the kids he'd seen had all seemed to have loud unfriendly voices, cycling round on old bikes like two-wheeled vultures, throwing tyres over lamp-posts, or squirting their names in aerosol over the bus shelter. No, the place wasn't at all the way he'd pictured it when his dad had broken the news to him.

'It's a little corner shop where we'll be our own bosses, work for ourselves. And it could turn out to be a little gold-mine, the fellow reckons; we could double the profits if we work hard. Got a nice modern house over it, too ...' 'Down Kent,' he'd said. It had sounded great. But Paul might have known. He'd passed through some pretty desolate places when they'd been out in the car, and this had to turn out to be one of them. And judging by an unguarded look on his mother's face from time to time, Paul reckoned she wasn't all that smitten either.

Feeling a bit sick, he forced down the last chocolate from its crinkly paper tray and threw the empty box to join the others on the top of his wardrobe. Living in a shop had some advantages! 'Don't eat the profits!' everyone had said. Well, what else was there to do? He'd get rid of all his empties in the dustbin later on; but no hurry, it'd be weeks before they all felt more settled and his mother would want to dust up on his wardrobe. Just now he'd have a wander around till the shop shut at one.

What took him to Victory Park that Sunday morning was partly aimlessness – he had to go somewhere – and partly the sudden excitement of the shouting. He'd heard it the second he'd put his head out of the side door. It had perked him up a bit for they were men's voices he could hear – loud, urgent, partisan – and he knew what it was all about as soon as he heard them: there was a football match on, and with a small crowd watching by the sounds of it. This might fill a bit of time till the shop was shut, he thought.

Houses and a high hedge cut off his view until he got to the park gates: but the excited shouting seemed to carry over the low roofs like fire sirens over a city, and he suddenly found himself running round the protective privet to see it before it could stop. He could picture the scene: twenty-two players in the middle with a ragged fringe of spectators all round the pitch. He saw it all the time in the park back home, when he and his dad – never satisfied, his mum said, with their Saturday afternoons at Spurs or Arsenal – would watch the local lads on Sunday mornings. This might be good. He always enjoyed a good game of football, with a cheerful crowd of keen supporters. But as he ran into the park he wondered where the devil they were hiding. The crowd had disappeared. There was still the shouting, but he could see only players, with just a couple of men on the touch-line and two kids kicking a ball about behind a goal.

Paul stopped, and the penny dropped. It didn't take a second; he wasn't daft. The shouts were coming from the

7

players themselves, calling for the ball, urging one another on, complaining to the ref., making enough noise for a small crowd.

'Ref*eree*!'

Fascinated, Paul stuck his hands in his pockets and walked up to the touch-line. They were big, these players; big, with red wet faces and legs like tree trunks. One team looked a bit like Spurs, dressed in white with dark blue shorts; very elegant, he thought. He hoped they were winning. The other team hadn't the same taste in strips; theirs consisted of washed-out red shirts and a variety of shorts, blue, white, black. But they were moving the ball about, creating space and opportunities to attack, looking dangerous. And all the time the shouting went on. As the reds swept forward, the number nine, making an early run, called for the swift ball that would give him five metres' advantage.

'Tommy, Tommy, Tommy, Tommy!'

He didn't get it; it was sent out to the left wing and lost into touch, but before he could complain someone else had smoothed things over with another shout, showing appreciation.

'Good call, Danny Smith!'

Paul walked further along the touch-line towards the centre-flag. It was good this, hearing the game so clearly. You could learn a lot about football standing here. But the referee chose that moment to blow his whistle, three short blasts and his hands held out to receive the ball, and Paul looked eagerly for signs that it wasn't the end, but only half-time. He could take another forty-five minutes of this without any bother. He watched to see where they would go.

Gathering in twos and threes the teams started to walk off the pitch, the reds towards a couple of men on the far touch-line, the whites towards Paul. Well, that was a good sign, neither of them making for the green corrugated hut behind the right-hand goal. Then the referee sat on the ball in the centre-circle and listened to his watches. Good. It was only half-time, then.

The reds grouped themselves over on the far side and here, where Paul was, the whites did the same, some sitting, some standing, one man flat on the ground with his arms above his head in surrender. But they were talking earnestly; there was no one running about and kicking a ball or jumping on people's backs like the kids did at half-time at school. One of the whites sliced some oranges on a paper bag while an older man in a faded black track-suit went round talking quietly to individuals.

'You've got that number three beat,' he said to a tall sandy-haired man with the reddest face Paul had ever seen. 'Now use it, son. 'E knows 'e's 'aving a stinker, so 'e's gonna get clumsier and rougher. So keep takin' 'im on — draw another man out o' the middle to cover 'im. *Then*, you release the ball. Right?'

Sandy-head just nodded, looking at the studded ground, and caught the piece of orange thrown at him. But it was not a sullen silence, more preoccupied, and he sank down to sit on the grass with his knees drawn up in front of him while he thought about the game.

Paul inched closer, fascinated, to hear more of this dressing-room talk. He noticed that the man in the track-suit just went round speaking to them individually, making shapes and movements with his hands in the air to emphasize his points; some nodded, some answered, some argued; but it was all quiet and very earnest. Paul wondered if it was like that in Spurs' dressing-room.

The talk away from the manager, among the players themselves, was louder.

'I want you out quicker when it's a goalie's ball,' the number five was saying to the number two. 'Push 'em up

9

when it's ours, for the off-side; come out quicker, then it's down to them to get back . . .' He sounded like the captain, a feeling which grew on Paul when he heard him talking next to the number four, a younger player who didn't look as red as the rest. 'Don't worry, son, you're doing all right. Ain't 'e lads?' There was a general murmur of agreement, low and breathless. 'Don't let that big feller worry you: 'e's done for! Second half you'll play 'im right out of the game. You'll 'ave Johnny Scott fighting to get 'is place back when 'e gets over getting married!'

'If she lets 'im play!' someone laughed from the grass.

Paul smiled. He could imagine how the absent player had had his leg pulled by the lads in the team. He could imagine the matey celebration that had taken place somewhere locally.

He looked down at the grass and he thought again of his own little gang of friends at school – at the old school. He thought of Simon Tulip, his best friend, and how welcome his familiar rallying cry would sound across this football field. 'All my men!' God, how he'd run to join him!

'Do us a favour, son.'

The voice cut into Paul's thoughts like a knife into a meringue, disintegrating them completely. 'Take the ref. a slice of orange. Keep 'im sweet for us . . .'

It was the man in the track-suit, the manager. On his flattened palm he held a slightly grubby quarter of orange. But already, as he proffered the fruit, he had half turned away to say something more to one of the players. Paul took the fruit without a word, and the manager looked back at him. 'Cheers,' the man said, very matter-of-fact. And, almost in the same breath, 'Now I want you to play wider this half, Roy. String out that defence an' it'll start to give – you see . . .'

Happy to have a sense of purpose at last, Paul ran on to

the pitch and over to the referee. Up close he looked very smart: a shiny nylon top that was black, not grey, with white collars and cuffs, and a pair of straight-seamed black socks with the end of a new pencil protruding from the top of each. He raised his eyebrows blandly at Paul.

'Orange?'

'Beg pardon?'

Paul held it up higher. 'Bit of orange?' He flicked his head backward. 'They sent it, over there. Whites . . .'

'Oh, yes.' The man almost took it. 'Well, no thank you, laddie. Tell them, "No, thanks." '

'Oh.' Paul shrugged. 'O.K.' He ran off faster than he'd run on. Funny, he thought; didn't he like orange, or did he have to be so impartial he wouldn't take a piece provided by one of the teams?

As Paul ran back the team was getting to its feet, stamping re-tied boots into the ground with new determination. The man with the sandy hair stubbed out a cigarette, and new chewing gum went into several mouths, the wrappings on to the pitch. The manager took one look at the orange in Paul's hand.

'No want?' he asked.

'No. He said, "Thank you" . . .'

'Please 'imself. You 'ave it then, son.'

'Ta.'

'Yeah, you 'ave it.' Then he shouted again. 'Remember, Roy, keep wide. And 'eads up, lads. We're not done yet . . .'

Paul tore the fruit off the thick peel with his teeth and put the whole quarter in. So they were losing. Well, he thought, you'd never have known it from the way they were talking; friendly, quietish, but with a sense of purpose. Not a bit like the excuses and the blamings you'd expect. No doubt about it, it was good, this: all these men with a common goal, the real one down there, and all the team effort they were making. To Paul, on his own and aware that he was missing the tight team spirit of his over-worked family, it seemed the answer to everything he wanted just now; and as he stood to watch the second half he felt an uncomfortable yearning to share some of it.

'Come on, Whites!' he suddenly found himself shouting.

But the second half was something of an anticlimax. Clear attacking moves were few, and the ball seemed to spend more time being fetched from over the touch-line than it did in play. Fairly, the game ended in a draw, although whites' equalizer was little satisfaction from a football point of view. It was an unfortunate own-goal that left reds' goalkeeper down in the dumps. But through-out the second half the shouting had gone on, the playing for one another, the urgent advice. Sometimes it was shouted in exasperation, occasionally a gloating cry – 'Oh, nicely, son!' – more to rile a beaten man than to con-gratulate the victor; but it all left its mark on Paul. As they trooped off to the green corrugated changing-hut together, he would have given anything to go with them. He desperately felt the need to be part of something like that team.

The idea, when it came to him, seemed too obviously simple for words. He'd join a team like that himself! Or even start one. Boys his own age, of course. But there were bound to be people around who'd play in a team if it was organized – there were a couple of kids down behind the goal for a start – especially if the team had a good leader, someone who could talk to them like that bloke in the track-suit. Simon Tulip was the sort who could do it. Perhaps there was someone like him down here, who ran things. Paul would willingly fall in behind anyone who'd got a team, or who'd get one going. Like at school; he'd always fitted in all right. His heart quickened slightly with anticipation when he suddenly thought about school. The school team! Of course! He'd be a fourth-year now, and if he could make the team there'd be a ready-made set-up for him: a bit of friendship, and a chance to show what he could do with a ball, just like these men here.

So now he knew; he knew what he wanted; he knew what might make life bearable out here at the back-of-beyond. And he was handy enough with a football to do it, he reckoned.

'All my men!' Wouldn't it be great to hear that shout in the playground down here – whether it was Simon Tulip shouting it or some local kid. Well, who knew what would happen next day? At least he had a plan, he began to tell himself.

There was an extra pressure of purpose on the pavement as he ran back to the shop, and while he listened to his parents' tired conversation about the morning's trade a glimmering spark of enthusiasm was beginning to kindle.

'Have you had enough, Paul?' his mother asked him as he forked the last of the peas off his dinner plate.

'I'm not sure,' said Paul, intentionally seeing a double meaning to her question. Earlier, when he'd been miserably cooped up in his bed, he'd been wanting to go back to the old home as eagerly as a racing pigeon on a desolate railway platform. But now he knew what he wanted if he were to make anything out of staying, and he decided he was prepared to circle the place for a bit, try out his wings, before he passed final judgement.

Nothing to lose, he thought, as the plate was replaced by a tub of cold mousse.

Chapter Two

PAUL needed a ball, a good new one, sparkling white and asking to be kicked, the sort you couldn't leave alone even when it was in its string bag. Always the best way into any game was to have your own gear; it made you independent and it gave you a permit to play. Of course, he wouldn't be the only one with a ball, but if it was smart and new he'd stand a good chance of having it used. And getting-in in the playground was the first vital step to getting into the team.

Paul had seen the ideal thing in the shop. In the far corner there was a small toy section, mostly cheap plastic odds and ends, but there was a good ball there, a Cup Final Special, regulation weight and in thick white moulded plastic. He'd eyed it before, but with no one to play with it had been pointless asking for it. Now he knew he needed it. He hadn't seen the price, but he guessed it wouldn't be cheap, even to his parents. He didn't think they'd refuse it to him. Although they were so tired and busy that they didn't know whether they were coming or going, they were both feeling a bit guilty about leaving him to his own devices, so he felt pretty confident he'd be given it if he asked. It was just a question of actually getting it in his hands: then he could really begin to feel happier about the first day of term.

Maureen Daines was in the hall, checking off some boxes. Norman Daines was in the shop, up a creaking pair of steps, putting Shredded Wheat on a high shelf. It was like every evening behind the shop's closed doors, the pair of them hard at it and too busy even to pretend an interest in the old things, like a favourite television programme or a football score. Even watching the box wasn't much fun on your own, Paul had found, without your dad sitting up at the girls on the adverts, or your mum sparkling with a secret smile at one of the young men. All the fun went when you couldn't share it. So Paul left the television flickering at the piled boxes on the settee and sauntered out into the hall to ask for the ball.

It almost pained his mother to be reminded of his presence. She winced when she saw him, not so much at him as at herself, and she put the checking list on the top box under a kitchen knife.

'Oh, yes, Paul,' she said, as if she'd been planning to say this all along and Paul's sudden appearance was all she'd been waiting for; 'have you got everything you need for the morning? Plimsolls, shorts, felt-tips, that sort of thing?'

'Yes, I've packed my duffel-bag.' There was everything he'd need in there, including a free box of chewing gum at the bottom.

'Good.' She pushed the hair back out of her eyes, tucking it behind her ears, regardless of her appearance. 'I've got new socks and jeans for you, and you can wear your best denim top ...'

'O.K.'

'And I'll come up with you and see you settled, like he said in the letter. So don't worry about that. Dad'll have to cope to start with ...'

'O.K. Mum ...' The ball. That new ball was going to be very important.

'Yes?' She had already turned away, was already sizing up the next box to be opened.

'Tomorrow ...'

But he got no further. From the shop there was a sharp crack and a wobbly yell, and the air was suddenly filled with the sound of falling boxes and packets and the dull

ring of tins on metal display stands. It sounded cata-
strophic. But the following shout was the worst, the long,
offended, and frustrated agony of it.

'Oh, God, NO!'

'Norman ...' She was in the shop before the last can
had stopped rolling.

Paul followed her like the ambulance behind the fire
engine. His father was lying behind the counter beneath a
mountain of Shredded Wheats, cake mixes and Chinese
dinners, while the shelf they had stood on hung sloping
forward on bent brackets, jammed against the collapsed
display stand of tinned custard.

It was a comic sight. In a film it would have been a
hilarious incident. But there was no comedy in this.
Maureen Daines helped her husband to his feet, dusting
rice out of his hair, trying to soothe the angry inflamma-
tion of his language with the ointment of sympathy.

Paul picked up a can or two and stood them on the
counter; but there was little help he felt he could give at
that moment, for his tired father had suddenly turned his
back in a vain attempt to hide the tears of his frustration,
and he was motioning help away with urgent backward
gestures of his hands. Paul wasn't wanted there. This was
private. It upset Paul, made him feel uncomfortable, but
it had to be sorted out by just the two of them.

So he made a quiet exit to his bedroom, with the ball he
wanted held tightly in his hand.

Chapter Three

AN attempt had been made to make the first prefabricated stage of Cherry Tree Primary School look as if
it belonged by rooting it into the stony soil with rose beds
and by putting prickly child-proof shrubs under the walls;
but the real work of marrying it in with the modern brick
extension had been done by the drifting clouds of local
cement dust which fell out over the whole estate like fine
snow. It reduced all the buildings to a grey monotony,
until they all matched. Against this background it took a
strong sun to pick out any individuality, whether it was of
architecture or of dress.

It was the first thing Paul noticed about the populated
school, the grey same-ness of everything, the pale faces,
the neutral clothing, the flat voices carried away by the
prevailing wind. It contrasted strongly with what he'd
known at the other school – bright colours, sharp accents,
spiced breath – and it suddenly seemed to offer hope to a
lad from London. With all the older kids off at the Com-
prehensive in Eastfleet, there shouldn't be too much
trouble in establishing himself in this little lot. They'd
probably welcome a good ball player into the school team
with open arms.

He didn't like to look from side to side too much as his
mother walked with him across the playground, but he
thought he saw one or two signs of notice being taken of
them, and he certainly heard the words 'new kid' and
someone say, 'Jobbers' Shop'. How long before the shop
was known as 'Daineses'? he wondered. But on the first
day of the school year everyone is chiefly occupied with

his own thoughts of what might lie in store, and there were no signs of him being either welcome or unwanted as he passed through. Before he knew it, Paul was inside the clean bare school, standing beside his seated mother outside the headmaster's room.

The blue door of the headmaster's room opened and a youngish man in a dark suit ushered out a mother with a very unhappy looking infant. With a smile and a word of reassurance he handed the boy over to the welfare assistant, then he called in the next of several waiting parents.

After twenty minutes Paul's mother began to get edgy. There were still several infants to enrol. She looked up at the wall clock when it gave its next jump forward, and she pointedly checked it against her own watch.

'I didn't think we'd be ten minutes,' she said, a little over-loudly. 'Monday's murder and Dad's coping in the shop on his own . . .'

Paul knew she was hoping one of the mothers in front of them would invite them to go next; but no one said a word, except in a very preoccupied way to their children; and both the Daineses were too new to ask.

The flow into the infant class was regular; but each admission took time, and every minute further divided Mrs Daines' loyalties into two. She knew she had to wait with Paul. Yet she wanted desperately to be back at the shop, helping to cope with the queue to the door. But at last their turn came and the headmaster, smiling warmly, ushered them into the teak and textile austerity of his office. They each sat on a curly-piled lemon chair facing the smooth expanse of desk, while the headmaster went round behind it.

'You don't mind if I smoke?' he asked, sitting on his swivel chair.

Mrs Daines shook her head, surprised. Of course not, it was his office, wasn't it?

'Good,' he said, lighting a small cigar and coughing on it. 'First day back's a bit hard after three weeks on the Italian Riviera! I was going to give these up, except I found I'd bought fifty instead of five on the boat! However, that's neither here nor there, is it, er,' he looked at a list in front of him, 'Paul?'

Paul shook his head. This man was another surprise, another difference to make him feel out of touch. He seemed far too young to be a headmaster. And fancy telling them about his holiday.

'You've got the shop, eh? A schoolboy's dream of heaven, living in a sweet shop. You're not eating all the profits, I hope?'

He smiled, and Paul vigorously shook his head, aware of his reddening face. Why did everyone have to say that?

'It's not just sweets,' Mrs Daines broke in. 'It's a general stores. We sell all sorts . . .'

'Ah, well, I know where to come in a shortage, eh?'

He turned back to Paul as Mrs Daines willed herself not to look at her watch. This was taking far too long.

'And you've moved here from North London? Well, I won't ask you what you think of Eastfleet yet. It's early days, and I might get a rude answer! Anyway, Paul, I'll be getting your records from your old school, and I'm sure you'll settle into your new class here without any bother. It's a bit more difficult for a big chap like you, coming into the fourth year; but you're not a baby, and your class has got a new teacher, so everyone will be finding their feet together. Now, Paul,' he leaned forward, 'if you're not happy, in any trouble, got any problems, don't hesitate to come to me. The name's Griffiths.' He smiled. 'Steve Griffiths.'

'Yes, sir,' said Paul.

'Good. And just remember, no problem's too big, and no problem's too small.' He turned back to Mrs Daines. 'Now, I've got his date of birth, his father's name, and his address, all in your letter.' He referred to the small sheet of blue paper before looking up with a smile. 'So that's about it, thank you, folks . . .' He pushed himself back on his casters – a practised movement – and he stood up, giving his chair a jaunty spin before walking round his desk to join them.

'Now, I expect you'd like to see his class . . .'

This time Mrs Daines did look at the clock. 'Will it take long?' she asked. 'Only my husband's on his own in the shop . . .'

'Well, some other time, then. Perhaps you can meet him from school one afternoon . . .'

'Yes . . .' But she doubted it. After school would be their busy time. 'There'll be an open evening won't there? When his dad and I can both come up?'

'Oh, yes.' Mr Griffiths tucked his fingers in his waist-coat pockets. 'You'll be getting a letter sent home about all that.'

'Yes.'

'O.K. then, Paul? Now we'll go and meet Miss Simmonds, and your mum can get back to help relieve the siege at the shop!' Laughing, he led the way out of his room, shook hands with Mrs Daines, and started to walk swiftly down the corridor, one hand in his trouser pocket, the other placed confidently on Paul's shoulder. 'And what position do you play?' he asked, not really wanting a reply. 'Midfield schemer? I like the sound of that. That always seems to be the brains of the team, from what people tell me. But I wouldn't know. I hate to admit it, but I'm a rugby man myself . . .'

They could hear Paul's class before they were within two rooms of it. Mr Griffiths quickened his pace to get there ahead of the boy and he burst unceremoniously through the door as a high-pitched female yell shrieked in exasperation.

'*Shut up!*'

Paul, following the headmaster through the door, cursed his luck for being associated with the force of law and order.

'Be quiet! This is a disgraceful display!' Mr Griffiths' hands were on his hips, his feet apart, as he gave the room a few seconds to quieten. 'You must have reading books in your desks you can be looking at while Miss Simmonds does the dinner register!' He glowered at the class, who were sitting at clear, freshly polished, and very empty desks. 'Well?' Mr Griffiths waited for a move towards reading, for a book to appear. 'I'm waiting ...' But although desks opened and closed for effect, there was nothing in them for anyone to produce.

'Please sir, we ain't sir.'

The voice came from the rear of the class, no hand or body raised to indicate the speaker. But Mr Griffiths obviously recognized him.

'Haven't, Billy. Not *ain't*. You *haven't* got books, is that it?'

'Yeah. We '*aven't* got books.'

Mr Griffiths turned to the young woman who was seated at the teacher's desk.

'I was going to give them out in a minute,' she said, standing up. 'But Mrs Daniels wants the dinner numbers as soon as possible.'

'I know she does.' Mr Griffiths said no more to her. But he turned his displeasure on the class. 'All right, I know Mr Moore isn't here. But we're very grateful to Miss Simmonds for coming here from St Joseph's to take you this year while he's away on his course. You must help her, though. She doesn't know all our ways, and I depend on you to help, not to let yourselves down by stupid behaviour. You're fourth years now, in case you've forgotten it, and I expect a certain standard from fourth years.' The

21

headmaster looked round the silent room and lowered his voice, gesturing dramatically towards Paul. 'What's our new friend to think of us? He's come from a big school in London where I'm sure the standard of behaviour is better than you've demonstrated this morning. What must he think?' He turned to Paul in a display of mock apology. 'Paul, I hope you can forgive your new colleagues for this poor start. I assure you it is not at all typical of Cherry Tree School . . .'

Paul didn't know what to say, so he kept quiet. His heart was in his boots, though. What a start. What a good way to be introduced to a new class. What a popular figure he was going to be after this! He knew what it was like. You hated people's guts for something like this.

'Well, I'm going to leave you to it. Wendy and Sharon, give out the *Wide Range Readers*. If they're too easy, read them fast, for speed and ideas. If they're too hard, look at the pictures and think up what words you'd put underneath. But do *something* for the next ten minutes, and I'm coming back to see how you're getting on! Thank you, Miss Simmonds.'

With that he went out, all his bounce gone, his summer holiday fading with the tan beneath his suit, and he left Paul standing at the front like a man who'd got off the train that had just left the platform. But Paul was determined to try to retrieve the situation somehow. As Miss Simmonds gestured him to a free space at a group of four desks near the front, he held up the bright new football which shone through its net bag.

'Please, Miss, what shall I do with this?'

It was an unfortunate choice of words.

'Don't tell 'im, Miss! Don't tell 'im!'

It was Billy from the back, and once more the class was in an uproar which Miss Simmonds couldn't quell. She snatched the ball from Paul and put it on an obvious cupboard top, behind several other balls, and Paul sat miserably down. He looked cautiously round the room. At least he knew who he had to get in with. That boy Billy. With a rugby-loving head, a teacher you could play up, and no Simon Tulip, it was Billy whose man he'd have to be.

The first break-time at a new school tells you all you need to know. Paul sensed that as soon as he got out into the air. In a classroom there are undercurrents, indications, smiles across the aisles or fists under the desks; but it isn't until you get outside and conversation is unrestricted that you begin to learn where you stand, what you lack, and what you need to do to make life bearable. Simon Tulip had been in the enviable position of doing the choosing, calling the tune, at the other school, and Paul had been his best friend. Here there was Billy, and Paul knew he'd have to use all his experience to decide what Billy was all about.

For the past hour-and-a-half Paul had been sitting in a group with two talkative girls and a silent partner who wrote 'Arthur Little' on his new books, and he had kept his peace while Billy and some others had run rude rings round Miss Simmonds, calling out, laughing when it pleased them, burping and saying loud pardons. It had been a big relief when an electric buzzer had sounded for break-time and the class had scrambled for the door, oblivious to Miss Simmonds' shouts. Paul had quickly separated himself from his group and followed the jostling crowd towards the playground, his ball held tightly in his arms.

Once outside a few younger children gave him a second glance as they ran past to form their groups and start their games. But of the boys in his own class there was no sign at first, until the sight of an arching ball above the asbestos kitchen told him there was a playing space beyond. He tried to walk round to it, but impatience forced him into a run, to stop just short of the corner, and, with a carefully prepared expression, neither over-eager nor too tightly closed, to stroll casually round.

The game was being played against a short length of clear brick wall upon which a small goal had been painted, with the unnecessary word GOAL in the centre. The teams were exclusively boys from his own class, with Billy between the flat whitewashed posts. It was a one-ended game, attackers and defenders playing into the one goal, and Billy seemed to be dominating it, loudly claiming every ball remotely within reach as his.

Paul stopped and put his own ball on the ground between his feet. With Billy being kept so busy, there'd be no chance of being invited into this.

They weren't all that good, Paul decided; if these boys were to be in the school team then he should make it, too. But Billy was a skilful goalie, and it was obvious that the whole game was organized the way it was purely for his benefit. When the three goals had been scored (Paul noticed that it took five to get three, since Billy disallowed two good goals as being on the post) the attackers and the defenders changed position, but Billy remained in the goal. It was a good job he played on pitch himself, Paul thought. There'd be no competing with this boy.

Billy was tall without being skinny, athletic looking, and smartly dressed in a red track-suit top and jeans. He had the sort of fair hair that didn't ruffle in the heat of the game, but fell back into place naturally, and only his reddening face gave an indication of his strenuous exertions to keep the ball out. The shouting did that, too, calling the odds, abusing the other boys for poor play, the tirade of words issuing from a thin mouth that twisted them out as if what he was shouting was really meant to be confidential. It was as if he was confiding his disgust in them at the top of his voice. The others, probably having given in to him since they'd first been infants, allowed him his own way in all things, apologizing for bad balls when Billy couldn't get to them, running and getting them for goalie's kicks when they went over the wall into the coke pile, complimenting him on almost every touch. Paul's spirits sank. He'd never get into this closed set-up! and even if he did, he was sure he couldn't take all that grovelling round Billy.

In no time the whistle went; Mrs Lewis, the senior infant teacher, no lover of boisterous break-times with the juniors, gave a specially loud blast round their private corner to get the fourth-year game to end. But Paul decided to stay where he was for a moment. Billy would have to walk past him to get into school, and a sort of fatal fascination held Paul there to see what would happen. The tall boy could either walk past him, absorbed with his group, and pretend not to see him, or he could stop and say something, perhaps try to recruit a new follower.

With his own red ball under his arm Billy came towards him, listening to someone complimenting him on a save. It was clearly in his mind to ignore Paul, until he saw the ball in Paul's arms. It certainly took his eye up close. Still unkicked, it did look attractive, smooth white with sharp black lettering.

'That a Frido ball, son?' Without asking, he took it from Paul's hands and pressed it professionally with his thumbs, like a First Division goalie before a match.

'Yeah. Cup Final Special.' Paul didn't reach out to get it back. He dropped his hands and waited for Billy to finish admiring it.

Billy bounced it hard on the ground twice.

'Regulation weight?'

Paul nodded. 'Yeah. Proper ball, only plastic . . .' It

25

had been a good move, then, bringing the new ball.

Billy still held it. 'Thought so.' Then he suddenly changed the subject. 'Didn't I see you yesterday over the park?'

Paul nodded again. Billy must have been one of the boys kicking about behind the goal. Well, it had shown his own keenness in the game, watching the match to the end the way he had.

'Hanging round the other team, London Docks, wasn't you? Eating their oranges?'

Paul stared back at him. The *other* team? Did there always have to be a catch? How was he to know who was who? It hadn't been deliberate disloyalty to the estate.

'Thought so.'

Without warning, Billy dropped the ball at his feet and back-heeled it away from the group, back towards the vacant goal.

'Can't use that 'ere,' he said. 'Too 'eavy for the windows. School rule . . .'

He walked away in the midst of his giggling group, the king surrounded by his fawning court, self-important, confident in his leadership. Paul's spirits dropped into his boots as he walked over to get his ball. It was the final stoop to pick it up that got him, that made his eyes prick, like a beaten goalkeeper bending to retrieve it from the back of the net. He forced himself into a trot back into school, twenty metres behind the last girl, and as he ran he thought of the crowd that he would normally have been in, surrounding Simon Tulip. He thought of the gaggle of laughs, and the thumps, and the loud clever remarks — just what Billy was enjoying right now.

And suddenly he wanted it back like he'd never wanted anything in his life.

Chapter Four

PAUL had heard his Uncle Geoff, the soldier in Ireland, call it *keeping a low profile*, the business of keeping your head down, not presenting yourself as a target. When he thought about it Paul realized he'd been doing it ever since the family had moved to Eastfleet. He hadn't made a lot of himself, like going out on a new bike and showing off to attract attention. For a start, he hadn't got one, but in any case it had been his own choice to be like the musk-rat in *Rikki-tikki-tavi*, hanging back in the shadows, staying close to the walls, leaving the open spaces to others. He had lain in bed, watched television, and quietly drifted around the house. But if all that had been keeping a low profile then he could only think of his behaviour at school for the rest of that disastrous first day as digging a hole and hiding in it.

On the few occasions when Paul had felt really unwell at school – his eyes widened with the rolling nausea of stomach pains or narrowed by the pressing throb of a headache – he had got through it by thinking how good it would be when his mother got home from work: there'd be drawn curtains, sympathetic words, and a car rug on the settee in front of the television. They'd always been close, their family, just the three of them, and Paul knew one or two – Auntie Marilyn for a start (with four kids) – who thought his mother was a bit soft on him at times. But today he had that same welcoming vision in front of him, and he knew that even Auntie Marilyn would agree he needed its comfort. His stomach ached with the feeling of being so unpleasantly excluded from things. All he wanted as he kept his head down was for three forty-five to come quickly so that he could get home. None of the new infants could have been waiting for home-time as desperately as Paul Daines.

He kept himself to himself and he got through the day by pretence. During lesson time he pretended to be completely absorbed in his work so that no one would want to disturb him – and that was no easy matter with the class in an uproar most of the day – and after a lonely school dinner with some younger children, he pretended all the midday break to be preoccupied with writing his name in ball-point on the unusable ball, crouching in a windy corner where the lolly papers rose and fell like sea-gulls, well away from Billy's game of football.

After one of the longest afternoons of his life the buzzer finally went. Paul was ready for it, his books closed in his hand waiting to be slipped inside his desk. He treated Miss Simmonds with calculated disregard, dived to the cupboard for his ball, and he was out of the door before the secretary's finger was off the buzzer button. He didn't want to bump into anybody who might prevent him from getting swiftly home to the comforts his mother would give.

The realization, when it came, hit him almost as hard as running smack into a brick wall. He was stupid, mental. All day long, when his thoughts had been of home, of deep-pile carpets and soft light and the tranquillizing bubble of gliding fish, it had been his old home he had seen in his mind, the London address, and he was half-way across the playground before the unfamiliar exit reminded him that it wasn't a real house he was going back to at all; it was a shop; and far from getting the sympathy he needed from his mother he'd probably have to queue up for her attention behind a shop-load of customers. He'd forgotten. Oh God! Everything was so blasted public in a shop. He was sharing his mum and dad with everyone else, and today, feeling lonely and low, he still wouldn't get near them. There wasn't a place where he could go for a bit of warmth.

He crossed over a featureless road, ran round a car jacked up on four piles of bricks in the kerb, and sprinted until he came in sight of the shop. Then he slowed to a walk. 'A. and F. Jobber' it said over one window; and, round the corner, over the other, 'General Provisions'. It would be strange to see their own name up, he thought. 'N. and M. Daines'. Or 'N. Daines and Son'. How about that in a few years' time? He followed the train of thought for a few moments, indulging himself in a few metres of day-dream. He saw himself behind the counter, taking money, working the till, having a chat. He'd have his place then. It was just rough that they wouldn't let him do it now. All the kids from school probably came in the shop; and you didn't get many boys from shops who were left out of everything. They weren't at the other school, anyhow. No, he'd like that; that could make a bit of difference. And Billy could take a running jump at himself then.

Norman and Maureen Daines were experiencing their third busy Monday in the shop. Mr Daines had just about recovered from his first school-morning rush, the shop packed with children buying sweets with their odd coppers, when the normal bustle of trade had begun, and after the first hectic hour on his own, he and Maureen had been kept going non-stop; twice she had slipped out to put a kettle on, and on the second occasion she had got as far as pouring the boiling water into the tea-pot; but they'd never got round to drinking it and before they knew it, it was twelve o'clock and the children going home from school filled the shop like wasps in a jam-pot with their dinner money change and anything else they had left over. And so it had gone on, and when Paul walked in through the shop door at ten minutes to four he was greeted by two parents who were rapidly changing their views about running the shop. They needed help, especially with the children; already the infants were dithering over the cheap confectionery, and the adults waiting to be served were prepared to be tolerant only up to a point: after all, they had food to buy and meals to cook. So the return to school had changed more than one outlook.

'Good, it's you, Paul,' his mother shouted. 'I want you to go out the back and wash your hands and give us a hand with the sweets and ices.' She had stopped in the action of sliding a tin of tobacco along the formica counter. 'Excuse me, Mrs, er . . .'

'Gosling, dear. No, go on. But remember you've took for that . . .'

'Yes, love, I know.' Mrs Daines blew a wisp of hair out of her eyes with an upward puff from her lower lip. 'Paul, Dad's tried to put all the cheap sweets near the 'fridge this afternoon; you stand there; children who only want odds and ends can all be served in one place . . .'

Mr Daines was already at it, delving deep into the freezer and turning it all over for a packet of Whizz-pop lollies at the bottom. 'Yes, Paul; have a go son, for God's sake . . .' His famous smile, the one that crinkled his blue eyes and just turned up the ends of his soft moustache, the smile his friends had told him would earn him a fortune in business with the housewives, was fast being replaced by the grim bristle of fatigue, and a worried frown seemed to be becoming permanent. 'Put your money in the big till. Don't bother with the numbers, ring up "No Sale" to open the drawer. And do your best to get the change right . . .'

Paul could hardly believe his luck. The foul taste of the day dissolved when he heard the sweet news. Of course

he'd help. This was just what he'd wanted all along.
'O.K., won't be a sec ...' He moved sideways along the
back of the counter and hurried out through the door into
the house at the rear. This changed everything! He slung
his ball in its bag into a corner of the hall, and, taking the
stairs two at a time, he raced into the bathroom. With a
quick look in the mirror he smoothed his hair down with
two wet hands, dried them on the towel, and as an afterthought he rushed into the narrow lavatory and stood
using the bowl, talking to himself while he waited impatiently to be done. 'Just right, just the job. Anyone
want lollies? Come on, son, don't waste my time ...' By
not stopping to pull the chain he was down the stairs and
behind his part of the counter within two minutes of being
asked.

'Yes, mate?'

It was a small boy with a wrinkled nose whose two-
pence piece dangled nonchalantly from a hand resting on
the freezer.

' 'Old on, I'm making up my mind.'

Paul leant on the counter, his weight on one foot: he
waited. He knew what he ought to do: at the sweet shop
on the corner near the old house the man had always
asked you how much you had to spend, then he'd made
suggestions to help you; but Paul didn't quite have the
confidence to start doing that yet. Also, his dad was still
there, serving a girl and seeing him get started, and that
cramped his style a bit. So he waited.

' 'Ow much are the ice-pops?'

'Two p.' Paul leant forward to the open carton, his first
sale.

'I don't want one.' Paul put it back, tightening the
corner of his mouth to show a small degree of exasperation. 'I'll 'ave two p. o' football bubble gum.'

Paul reached behind him and took four slender packets

out of a cardboard box with a cut-out lid. For a second the
thought flashed through his mind of the box of Spearmint
in his school duffel-bag, forgotten and unused. But you
couldn't dwell on anything for long in a shop, he discovered.

'Cards.'

'Eh?'

'Four cards I'm s'posed to 'ave with these.'

'Oh yes . . .' Paul groped into the box again and took
out four sugar-sprinkled cards from the corner, each
carrying a bluey photograph of a famous player. He
hadn't taken any of these cheap gums yet so he didn't
know. Then he looked up inquiringly at the next in the
line, a boy just a bit younger than himself. He began to
feel quite practised already.

'Yes?'

' 'Ere, mate!'

Paul looked back at the little boy, who still hadn't gone
away. He sighed very audibly. If he thought he was
going to change any of the cards he'd got another think
coming.

'Yes?'

'Doncha want the money?'

'Oh, yeah, ta . . .' With a swiftly reddening face, and a
quick glance to see if his dad had noticed, he took the two
pence piece and went over to the till. His first customer
hadn't been such a marvellous success. But things were
bound to get better.

He had used the till before, of course. The very first
night after they had moved in he had stood and played
with it, ringing up amounts and seeing them pop up in the
window; then he had used it to add up sums, seeing them
come printed out on a strip of paper. He had played at
opening the drawer with a flourish and closing it with a
slam, just like the shopkeepers he knew, so he should really

have known not to stand too close; and he should have known how swiftly the drawer came shooting out. But in the excitement of serving he had forgotten, and as the drawer knocked him sharply in the chest he was pained more by the sniggering of the kids at the freezer than by the blow. He had no time to dwell on his embarrassment, though, for the shop was filling up with juniors now and he was about to have his first experience of being rushed off his feet.

He didn't do too badly, he thought: he served them with what they wanted, even the ones who spoke so low he felt stupid asking them 'Eh?' for the third time, and he only made one small mistake with change. But apart from that he didn't do too badly; the boys were blunt and the girls, especially a couple from his class, got the giggles. But he did all right – until the big problem came up like a shark out of calm water and took a large and painful bite at his self-esteem.

It was Billy again. Paul had been serving for about twenty minutes when the tall boy came in. The homeward rush of children had been tailing off, and there were more adults than children in the shop, keeping his parents busy, and Paul had just begun to wonder what he'd have for a little free snack to round things off, when he had been aware – he could put it no more definitely than that – of Billy's presence. Something had made him look up from the bars of Milk Tray he fancied to the direction of the clattering shop door.

And from that moment on, every word, every expression, every move, was photographed in his mind like a film.

Billy stood just inside the doorway, staring at him, and there could be no doubt in Paul's mind that he was the reason for Billy's visit. There was something about the way the other boy stood there, almost like the outlawed

33

cowboy who has just pushed in through the saloon doors, about to challenge the sheriff. He must have seen him through the window and come into have a boss, Paul thought. He shivered slightly, and he was instantly aware that it might have been seen, so he covered it with a jerky movement to straighten a jar of wine-gums. At the same time he eyed up the distance to the house door behind him. Could he make a quick exit look natural? But somehow pride prevented him from chickening out and pretending to carry something out of the shop. Besides, his dad or mum would see he was up to something, and they'd only go and say something out loud. So he stood his ground, and tried to look at the approaching Billy just as he'd looked at all the other kids from school.

By now Billy was at the freezer counter, and the only thing to do was to walk over to him. Paul couldn't really put a finger on the reason for being uneasy about Billy. All right, Billy had been unfriendly at morning break-time, but he'd *done* nothing really, had he? Not serious. Being a bit off and kicking his ball away didn't necessarily mean he was Paul's enemy for life, did it? It just could have been a joke, couldn't it?

'Wotcha.'

And he sounded friendly enough. Paul looked beyond him to see if any of his cronies were there, but they weren't; he was on his own. Paul relaxed a bit. Perhaps now the others weren't about he'd come to make friends. Perhaps that business had just been a bit of show in front of them at break-time. He knew the feeling: he'd done the same sort of thing himself with Simon Tulip.

'Wotcha,' Paul replied.

'You serving, are you?'

'Yeah.'

Billy leant on the freezer. 'Your shop, is it?'

Paul looked round to indicate his busy parents. 'Well, sort of ...'

'Oh, nice ...'

Billy's eyes roved along the shelf behind Paul where the more expensive bars and boxes were kept.

'You're all right for sweets, then?' He smiled with one side of his mouth and he slowly slipped a pound note out of his shirt pocket and held it up, folded, like a man about to buy a round of drinks.

'I s'pose so ...'

A long silence hung between them, and neither of them made the move to end it. In a new situation everything had to be played by ear: Paul felt instinctively that an awkward silence was to be preferred to a wrong word being spoken. It was like the first round of talks between two untrusting nations. You had to be so careful. And peace talks couldn't be hurried.

'Well now, what'll I have?'

Paul raised his eyebrows, but still he said nothing. He was prepared to serve the boy, but there'd certainly be no suggestions from him to invite a rebuff.

'I'll have a large fruit and nut, and one of them boxes of liquorice allsorts.' There was a slight pause. 'Please,' he added, with another brief smile.

Please. Well, that meant peace, didn't it? Perhaps he'd been right. Perhaps the playtime business *had* been for the others. Perhaps now that Billy knew who he was, knew about the shop and that, that he wasn't just any old new-comer to the district, he was going to do his best to make friends with him. Perhaps things were looking up.

'Anything else?' Paul put the chocolate and the liquorice allsorts on the freezer top. He smiled tightly. It was a relief to be having something approaching friendly dealings with this boy. Billy shook his head, and Paul held out his hand. 'That's thirty-five pence, then ...' Making this sort of contact was lucky, he decided. Lucky and important. It would definitely stand him in good stead tomorrow.

''Ere you are,' Billy said in a loud voice. 'The right money.' He held his closed hand over the freezer top.

Paul frowned. He was sure he'd seen a pound note there a minute before, but Billy must have put that back in his pocket and taken out the silver when he'd been getting the sweets off the shelf. He opened his palm to take the coins. Then he caught his breath when the closed hand opened and he saw what Billy was offering him.

Nothing. For a second he couldn't believe it. There was nothing there. The hand was empty, the finger-tips forming a beak shape and pecking at Paul's palm as if the two of them were playing shops in a corner of an infant classroom, just pretending.

Billy was staring hard at Paul. 'That's right, isn't it, mate? Thirty-five p?' He winked conspiratorially, at the same time giving the strong impression that Paul could 'take-it-or-leave-it'. 'O.K.?'

Paul started breathing again, hard and heavy as if he'd just run a hundred metres.

'Eh?'

So that was it. Billy wanted Paul to buy himself in. If Paul wanted to be counted amongst Billy's friends he had to be prepared to go along with this trick, this swindling. There was no other way Billy's action could be interpreted.

'Just a minute.'

Paul's brain worked computer-fast while he pretended to check the money he didn't have in his hand. Now, what choice had he got? The sweets were already down the front of Billy's track-suit top, so he couldn't play the same trick back and give him nothing in return. No, that was out. He could march straight up to his dad and tell him, say something like, 'That boy's got a bar of chocolate and a packet of liquorice allsorts, and he won't pay for them'; that would definitely be the strongest action to take, because his dad would probably either throw Billy out of the shop or force him to hand back the sweets. But Paul's heart thumped faster as he thought of doing that: it'd be out-and-out war from then on if he did, and he did have to go back to school tomorrow with this boy. What should he do? Desperately, with time against him, the boy standing there, he tried to think. Any second now his dad might turn round, or Billy might walk out of the shop with the sweets. Either way his dad would be bound to know he hadn't rung anything on the till. Hell, there was no sleeping on this problem. He pleased the boy, or he did right by the shop. He reported the trick to his father or he pretended to put Billy's money in the till. It was down to that. Knuckle-under to Billy or start a war with him.

Paul looked up quickly at the other boy's face, still staring hard at him across the top of the freezer, and he suddenly knew what he was going to do – and why. He was going to give in. For now. This once. This kid had the whole top class behind him; one-for-one Paul might have taken him on; but Paul against all Billy's men would be a very different matter. There was more to it even than that, though; a lot more. At the moment this kid held the key to what Paul wanted most – a bit of friendship – and without Billy's O.K. it couldn't happen. Why should Paul chuck it down the drain for thirty-five pence?

Paul stole a quick look round to make sure neither of his parents was too near the till. They weren't. His mind was clear now. But no way would he ever be manoeuvred into a position like this again.

'Ta,' he said. 'Just right.' And he walked over and rang up 'No Sale' on the machine, rattling the groove of ten p.'s with his empty fingers. He slammed the drawer shut.

Thank God, he'd got away with it – and it'd been much easier than he'd thought. Well, at least he'd pleased someone. But by the time he looked back to receive Billy's appreciative nod, or a smile, the boy had gone, and the shop door was crashing shut.

Ten minutes later Paul was lying on his bed, trying to persuade himself that he'd done the right thing. And it didn't take long for him to do so; to work out the real reason for having done it; the most acceptable reason. It was dead simple, really. In fact, he must have known it all along, down inside. It had only been right to play along with Billy because the only possible explanation for Billy's behaviour was that it was a joke. They'd been having him on. Probably all the other kids had been outside to see the fun. No one would have risked something like that if it hadn't been a joke. No one could think Paul was that much of a pushover.

He lay back, put his hands behind his head, and stared at the gloomy ceiling. Yes, he thought, it would have been rotten to tell on Billy when to have done so would have meant real trouble for him. His own dad certainly wouldn't have seen that it had been a sort of joke, and he might even have gone up to the school about it. But Paul decided to make sure he told Billy all this in the morning. He would let him see the true value of his cooperation.

He heaved a sigh of relief. In the shop, at the time, he hadn't seen the practical joke side of it, it had seemed too serious; but now he finally convinced himself that he could see Billy's motive: it was just a bit of a laugh, to give Paul a nasty moment.

Anyway, he was well initiated now. He'd take his plimsolls tomorrow, and an older, lighter, ball. After playing up to Billy's joke like that he surely wouldn't want for a place in the game at break-time. Then he'd show them what he could do! And kids soon let the teachers know who ought to play in school teams. So he'd be getting what he wanted all round.

With that consoling thought he ripped the transparent skin off a box of Maltesers, screwed it into a ball, and tossed it skilfully on to the top of his wardrobe.

Chapter Five

EAGERNESS and anticipation took Paul to school early the next morning. Along the road he was all eyes for a glimpse of Billy, and when he got through the gate he swiftly scanned the playground for him. What mood would he be in today? Had Paul read his motives accurately the night before? Had he paid for a place in Billy's gang? He carried his old red football, light and conforming to the school rules, in a plastic bag from the shop, and he felt now that he had done as much as he could to fulfil the conditions for membership. It would all be down to Billy after this.

It didn't take Paul long to find him in the usual place. Well before school, it seemed, Billy was running his private game behind the kitchen. The first high ball, rocketing over the rooftop like a signal flare, took Paul running towards the corner. The game might usually be full up with equal sides at break-time, he thought, but there would surely be room for him this early, before everyone had arrived. Nonchalantly, his hands in his pockets and the bag banging against his calf, he walked round the corner and leaned himself casually against the dusty pink wall.

There were only four boys there. Paul had been right. And they weren't playing the same game as the day before. They were kicking the ball at the goal in turns from a chalked penalty spot. Billy, of course, was in goal, dancing about in front of the painted wall – cheating, for a start, Paul thought; the goalkeeper's feet must be still when the ball is kicked for a penalty – but like the other boys he didn't see the necessity of pointing that out.

At first Paul thought it was intense concentration, the way Billy never looked his way, only at the ball and the man who had it, shouting his instructions to try a low one, or put it on his right. As the minutes passed, though, it seemed more like a deliberate way of excluding him, pretending he wasn't there. Nobody could be that engrossed. Paul stood still and watched him, and he suddenly realized that he'd even been dreaming about this boy; and, becoming angry with himself, he began to see that in doing so he had built Billy up into something bigger than he really was. He actually looked very ordinary this morning, much less tough, even a bit fancy in his full red track-suit. Paul was tempted to shout, 'Let's have a game, then, mate.' But he didn't. Something about this boy still held him back.

Then one of the others scored, with a hard and accurate shot low on Billy's weaker left side. The goalkeeper went bravely down on the tarmac, getting a hand to it but being so stretched that he hadn't the strength to deflect it. But no one shouted, Paul noticed. They all waited for Billy to say something.

'Tipped it round, didn't I?' he asked.

Everyone knew the answer was 'No'; but the replies Billy got were, 'Yeah, just about,' and 'Good save on to the post . . .'

Paul wanted to shout 'Goal!' at the top of his voice; but some natural caution stopped him. His time would come, he told himself. Get in first, then flex his muscles later, that was the best way of doing it. So, he stood and waited for the time to come when Billy would have to notice him.

Paul had almost given up when the moment came. He had got to a count of eighty in the final hundred he'd allowed himself when the ball was fisted out by Billy and came arching over to where Paul was standing. It lobbed the other boys, and no one seemed to be in a hurry to chase after it. Had Paul stood aside it would have bounced and hit the wall and gone rolling down into the big playground. He didn't stop to think about it. As it dipped towards the ground he shaped himself up, took a step forward, and caught it on the volley with his right instep. It could have gone anywhere. Volleys like that usually did, greeted with derision when they went high and wide or by wild cheers when they found the net. But as luck would have it, his shot went cracking towards the goal, high to Billy's right, and it hit the wall with a loud plastic plunk in the angle between the painted post and the cross-bar. A great goal! As the ball had shot towards him Billy hadn't moved at first, obviously thinking that a ball kicked by Paul wasn't to be taken seriously; but somewhere along its flight he must have decided to make an easy save of it, for he jumped to his right with as much graceful ease as he could muster, like an unflustered goal-keeper in a pre-match warm-up. But he was late off the ground and he missed the ball completely.

'Lucky!' shouted one of the shooters, trying to save Billy's face. But he only made matters worse.

'Waddya mean, "Lucky!"?' Billy snapped. 'No goal!' He ran out of his goal and over to Paul as if he were chasing the referee in high indignation, stopping abruptly in front of him with his hands on his hips. ''Ere, mate, that 'it the angle, didn't it?'

Only the wall stopped Paul from backing away from the other boy's blazing eyes, his face just a blink away from a flying fist. That missed save mattered desperately to Billy.

There was no pause, no moment of painful decision today. 'Yeah,' said Paul. 'It swerved out. You had it covered ...' It mattered to Paul, too. It mattered a lot, well worth a white lie. As soon as it had hit the wall inside the goal he wished it hadn't. It was one thing for him to

42

look good, but quite another to make the other kid look ridiculous.

Billy said nothing. He turned on his heels and walked back towards the goal, putting the matter beyond doubt. 'No bloody "lucky" about it. He missed!' He reached the goal and swung back round at his men again. 'An' get your own balls back next time they bounce over your 'eads! We ain't 'ere to give free kicks to any old wallie!'

They nodded, and grunted; and Paul, who had got the message too, walked off round the corner, churning inside with anger at what Billy had said; but worse than that, he was contemptuous of his own cowardice at what he hadn't.

Miss Simmonds had hardly slept the night before, and it showed. After the headmaster's few words with her following that poor start the day before she had decided to try something she was familiar with, and she had sat up late preparing work cards and assignments for the class, the sorts of things the children from her other school could do so well. But then, worn out, she couldn't sleep and she'd lain there, her legs jumping, while her mind went over everything that had happened the day before. And now, almost before she knew it, here she was back again, with the enemy trooping in for another day's skirmishing.

'There are assignment cards on every table, one between four,' she said over and over again as the children came sauntering or charging in. 'Paper's on the cupboard. Anything you don't understand, ask me.'

Some took notice and others didn't, and as Paul turned round from putting his bag on the cupboard top he saw Billy holding an assignment card up to the light, as if he expected to see the answers watermarked inside it.

' 'Ere, Miss,' he called out, 'there's a bit of card on my desk. Shall I chuck it in the basket?'

43

'NO!' Miss Simmonds could see ten minutes' work being ripped into fragments if she didn't act firmly. 'If you take the trouble to read it you'll see it has quite a bit to do with you!'

'Oh!' Billy sat down, still staring at the card with puzzled eyes, his frown deepening for the benefit of the rest of his table as he put on a studied interest.

The card on Paul's table was already being read. It was under the close scrutiny of the boy who had sat silently next to him the day before, while the girls who shared their table of four desks sat looking at two elderly library books. Paul's eyes wandered between them.

'Oh, hello,' said the one with curly black hair.

'Hello,' said the red-headed girl, looking at her friend and unsuccessfully trying to control a giggle.

'We'll have a look after Arthur, eh Reet?' Lorraine, the curly one, nodded across at the other boy.

'What?' Rita had controlled herself. 'Oh, yeah ...' She pulled a face at Arthur for Paul's benefit, then she reopened her library book and began reading immediately from the random page.

Paul wondered what to do for a moment. All round the room there was a high level of noise as people got to grips with the work, looking over shoulders, sliding the cards with a scrape and a spin across the desk tops, calling out stupid questions; but since they were mostly grouped with friends they put up united fronts, some friendly, some hostile. Only Paul's table with its best-friend girls and the self-contained Arthur seemed to be without an agreed policy over the work. And Arthur had the only card. Paul decided to give him a bit longer with it, to see if he would offer it round or make any suggestions about it. Then, if he didn't, he'd ask to see it. Meanwhile, he decided to read the book he'd read the day before.

He opened it at the beginning again, but before he

properly focussed his eyes on the small print he took one quick, important, look behind him. Whatever he was doing now, he had to know about that other kid, Billy Richardson.

There were lots of questions to answer. Paul couldn't make it out, that aggro in the playground before school. He'd kept his mouth shut about the shop, hadn't he? That deserved a bit of consideration from the leader of the gang, didn't it? Billy couldn't expect nicking that chocolate and those sweets to go by without Paul getting something in return, could he? So what was he playing at? What was he waiting for? And if he wasn't waiting to do anything, didn't he think Paul would have the guts to report him? But as Paul looked across the bent and turning heads at the other table his hopes of getting Billy worried nose-dived to the ground. Holding his work-card up in front of his face Billy was obviously telling the others all about the afternoon before and the trick he'd pulled in the busy shop, for there was a sudden burst of laughter as he mimed the empty hand, and four knowing looks sneered across the classroom at Paul. The rat! With his head pounding red with frustration Paul looked back at the blur of print before him. This definitely needed some careful thinking about.

'Here, you were in your shop last night.' It was the girl with the curly black hair. 'You served me, but you didn't say nothing. Were you shy?' Rita snorted again while Lorraine held Paul in a challenging gaze. 'You gave me ten p. change too much, but I thought if you won't speak I won't, so I kept it. D'you want it back?'

'No thanks.' He remembered her now. She'd taken ages to buy a small bag of Treets. Quickly, to avoid further involvement, he turned to Arthur. 'What's on the card, mate? Anything interesting?'

'Oh, be like that, then!' said Lorraine. 'But don't forget

we wanna look, after you *men* have finished!' She flashed a wide-eyed annoyed look at Paul and turned back to her own book.

'Eh?' said Arthur. But his attention was on the card again.

Paul looked closely at Arthur for the first time. He was the sort of boy you noticed last, Paul thought, not being very big and with one of those concentrating faces that didn't seem to want to meet you half-way. Boys like him usually wore glasses. Arthur didn't, though, and their absence, if you got close enough, revealed a pair of green eyes set narrowly above a long straight nose, which gave him a piercing, inquisitive, look – when he bothered to look at anyone. With his light brown hair neither long nor short, and his old-fashioned jacket with odd buttons – he wasn't exactly an eye-catcher. And with an unimpressive name like Arthur Little on his books he seemed pretty nondescript all round.

At the moment he was looking round at Paul, perhaps aware that he'd been asked something but not certain what.

'The card,' Paul repeated. 'Much to do, is there?'

'Have a look,' said Arthur in a neutral sort of voice. He turned the card round for Paul to see, but he kept a grip on it himself.

Paul read it. It was like some of the stuff they'd done at the other school.

We are surrounded by NAMES. Our school is Cherry Tree Primary, on the CHERRY TREE ESTATE. The estate is on the outskirts of EASTFLEET.

Why are these places so named?

The roads on the estate have names, like ORCHARD AVENUE, TOLLGATE LANE, ASTRA DRIVE. The park is called VICTORY PARK.

The two public houses have names.

Make a list of as many proper names connected with the area as you can, starting with the road or the flats where you live. Use a local street map to help you (see me).

Some of these names may have special historical or geographical meanings. Can you find out something about them?

'Well, there's two answers to that,' Paul said in an attempt to be friendly: 'One'll take all week, and the other's "No"!'

Arthur said nothing, drawing the card back from Paul with a firm pressure. He obviously wasn't prepared to do any humouring. Still silent, and still clutching the card, he got up and walked over to Miss Simmonds, who was frantically trying to sort out a jostling group by the desk.

''Ere, 'e's only gone off with the card!' Rita with the red hair exploded in a high voice. ''Ow we s'posed to get our work done, then?'

'Not our fault then, is it?' Lorraine said. 'Anyway, she won't notice, I don't reckon. I'm gonna draw some fashions in a minute...'

Paul didn't want to draw fashions, though, and he began to wish he'd been more constructive about the card with Arthur. It would have been something to get on with.

'What was it, then? What we got to do?' Rita wasn't going to let go. 'It's got Little Arthur all excited...'

'Oh, it's just names,' Paul volunteered. 'Round here. We've got to find out why they're called what they are. That's all.' Paul didn't know why he had to be so off-hand about it; perhaps it was because he half expected a smart reply.

'That's easy, then,' said Rita with a nudge at Lorraine. 'I'll do Love Lane!'

'It's not its proper name,' Lorraine replied. 'You'll get nought out of a hundred for that!'

Paul put his head in the desk, ostrich-like, to dis-associate himself from the noise of their giggling. But in a way he envied those two girls. Their banter sounded very much like his own and Simon Tulip's in the old days. Miss Simmonds was shouting something at Billy, though, and Paul needn't have bothered to hide. When the shout brought him out, Arthur was there with a brand-new street map, crackling in its sharp folds as he spread it on his desk; but it was too big for his territory alone, and since the map overlapped on to Paul's, Paul suddenly had to be involved.

'If you and I do the estate and the streets,' Arthur said, 'they can do the pubs and the odds and ends . . .'

His voice was patient, but decided, and Paul could see no point in arguing. Anyway it seemed to be a reasonable idea.

'Oh, thanks a lot,' Lorraine put in. 'P'raps you'll let us have a look at the card, then.'

Arthur stared across the table at her with his sharp green eyes before silently handing her the assignment.

'Oh, don't force yourself!' Rita snatched it from him suddenly. But the impatience was only acted, and as the two girls put their heads together they tried to keep straight faces, looking at the card with Arthur watching. They had to turn it a couple of times to get it the right way up.

'Come on,' said Arthur. 'We can work in the school library. I got permission . . .'

Paul was only too pleased to agree. But as he stood up and self-consciously made his way to the classroom door, he couldn't resist a last look across at Billy Richardson. And he didn't know whether to be pleased or sorry that Billy was already staring hard at him.

Chapter Six

'No real need to be in here at all,' said Arthur. 'Not much call for books on this project, I wouldn't have thought; but we're better off out of that racket in the classroom.'

Paul agreed with him by his silence. The way Arthur put it somehow made him feel unsure of saying too much himself. But Arthur was right. They could sit down and just write answers to most of the stuff on the card. And it was certainly a treat to be in the library after the chaos of the classroom.

It was a small, well-organized room, and there was a certain sense of peace in here that was lacking where they'd just come from.

'Why don't you clear that vase off,' said Arthur, 'then we can work on the table.'

Paul, still silent, obeyed the command. He put the square stoneware vase of cornflowers on a shelf top and then stood by while Arthur, with carefully precise hands, spread the map on a low circular table in the middle of the room. Arthur beckoned for Paul to pull up a chair next to him – and he was obviously just about to announce that work would begin – when his right index finger suddenly pecked sharply at the map.

'Believe it or not,' he said, 'she's bought this herself . . .' He held his finger still while Paul did what Arthur wanted and took a close look at the neat rounded signature of ownership. *B. Simmonds.* 'Thirty-two pence, just for us.'

'Yes,' said Paul, called upon to speak at last. But that was all. He wanted to add something else, about it being generous, or daft, but once more he didn't feel able to.

'Are you a quick writer?' Arthur inquired, obviously not wanting to delay getting started.

'I dunno,' Paul had never asked himself the question.

'Well, there's quick scribbling for making notes, and slow neatness for best: only some people can't switch from one to the other. They're always either quick or slow . . .'

'I'm quick but not neat,' Paul jumped in, 'unless I have to be.' He wasn't going to be totally outdone by Arthur.

'Good, because I'm best at thinking aloud with this sort of work. You can jot it down, then we'll make a fair copy later . . .'

'O.K.' Reduced to being the secretary, Paul sat with his pencil ready and looked over the card which Arthur was still holding possessively. He didn't feel very happy about the way this was working out so far, but at least he was doing something *with* someone, and that awful feeling of being alone that he'd experienced for the past two and a bit weeks had gone for a little while.

'All right,' said Arthur, 'here we go . . .' He put on a frown of concentration and pinched the top of his nose with his fingers – for his benefit, Paul suspected, because the first part of the assignment didn't need much brain power.

'Well, let's take a few of these names off the map as I find them. It shouldn't be too difficult. Here's an easy one first. "Cherry Tree Estate".'

Paul nodded and looked at Arthur, waiting for the next bit, the explanation. It was easy, but it might as well be said.

'Well go on then, write it down.'

'Oh, yes . . .' Paul started scribbling the words, his mind buzzing with annoyance. Who did this kid think he was? Cheeky lank! '*Go on then, write it down!*' Paul wouldn't have looked at him at the other school; he and Simon Tulip wouldn't have gone within a thousand miles of him; yet here he was dishing out his orders! Paul finished writing and looked up. Any minute now he'd give him a right mouthful.

'Well, why do *you* reckon? I'm not doing all the work, you know ...'

Arthur was staring hard at Paul with his green eyes, his arms folded smugly in front of him like some teacher sitting at his table.

'Er ...' Paul turned an angry red, but he bit his lip. The snobby kid hadn't done any of the work so far; and any second now he'd tell him so, too; but some sense of uncertainty just held him back. But only just. Who did he think he was impressing anyway? This was hardly *Mastermind* stuff to someone whose dad knew every country lane round London. He decided to play along for a few minutes more. Flatly, certainly, he said, 'Because this was all cherry orchards once, before they built the estate.' You didn't need two heads for this. It was the only possible explanation, even if it hardly seemed possible, looking at the place today. He started to write, expecting a comment from Arthur, adding to what he'd said, or contradicting him – but when he had finished writing the sentence he looked up to find Arthur waiting with one finger pointing to the next place-name he had chosen.

' "Orchard Road" – same answer.' His finger moved impatiently once he'd said it, and he skewed the map round to read the next name more easily. ' "Tollgate Lane".'

Paul carried on writing from the last answer to put the new name down; this was giving him no time to plan a counter-attack, to decide what to say or what to do, but he was determined Arthur was going to take the responsibility for this one.

Perhaps Arthur sensed this; or perhaps he just wanted to show off; whatever the reason he began to give the answer at dictation speed without any hesitation, for Paul to write it down.

'Tollgate Lane ... goes from the estate ... to the main road ... where there used ... to be ... a crossroads ... and a tollgate. In the old days ... people paid ... to use the road. ... like they do now ... going through ... the Dartford Tunnel.'

Arthur stopped and nonchalantly looked at the map while Paul's stomach muscles fought a strange empty sort of feeling inside. It had been a good answer, that was the trouble, and Paul knew it was better than anything he'd have managed, especially the last bit, linking it with modern times. His dislike of Arthur began to grow.

' "Victory Park".'

Paul's pencil scribbled on. His fingers were aching. This was getting to be hard work. Another couple of answers and he'd jag it in and let Arthur do a bit of the sweat. But for the moment there was something else he had to do. Doing his best now to sound like the other boy, mouthing it slowly while he wrote it himself, Paul took over the next answer.

'Victory Park ... gets ... its ... name ... from ... the ... word ... "Victory" ... meaning ... when ... we ... won ... the ... war.'

Paul finished it and steeled himself not to look up at Arthur for approval. You had to be as confident as the other bloke at a time like this, he decided. But had he looked up, instead of embellishing the final full-stop with curls, he'd have seen Arthur vigorously rubbing his fringe from side to side, showing a real uncertainty at last.

' "Doran House",' Arthur said after a long pause, by which time Paul's full-stop had become a football. 'I only live there, and I haven't the least idea what the flats are called after. But it's someone's name, a million to one.'

Paul put on his own puzzled intellectual frown as the

break-time buzzer sounded. Then his moment came. He scored the point he'd been wanting to score ever since they'd come into the library. Arthur's uncertainty had to be punished after all *he'd* taken.

'Perhaps we ought to look it up,' he said, sounding a bit like the other boy as he broadly indicated the colourful row of books. 'After all, I believe that's why we came in here . . .'

But Arthur wasn't going to be put down that easily. 'Yes,' he said quickly, 'I was thinking that, too. Shall we stay in and do it now?'

Paul swore to himself and stood up. Arthur had turned the tables back again. He might have known Paul wouldn't want to stay in.

'No,' he said quickly, 'better still, let's have a breather. It'll do us good. I'll give you a kick-about instead.' He had to get out there somehow.

'All right,' Arthur said, 'but I'm not much good. I'm no Billy Richardson.'

Paul couldn't be sure whether Arthur's sharp look had any meaning or not, but he ignored it. 'Don't matter,' he said. And lost for further words again, he led the way silently out of the library.

Arthur was a terrible footballer. Paul found a place to play, just within sight of Billy's goal, but it was a gusty corner, where everything went chasing round in circles, and Paul's light ball and Arthur were no exceptions. Arthur was so bad that Paul began to realize how friendly the boy was prepared to be by agreeing to play in the first place. This sort of physical activity, combining the skills of eye and foot, timing, balance, control, was not natural to Arthur, and the more he tried to improve the worse he became. There were just the two of them passing the ball to one another, with Paul shrugging off a couple of attempts by younger boys to get into the game, but even simple returns of the ball were too much for Arthur. If the ball came at head height he would go up to head it, but mistime his jump so badly that he was down on the ground before the ball sailed over him. If it came along the ground, at whatever angle, he would take a first-time kick like a toddler, without attempting to control it first. If he tried to turn with the ball and dribble it, his turning circle was as wide as the school itself, and the ball was accidentally kicked off at frustrating tangents for minutes at a time. So the pair of them spent a great deal of time just retrieving the ball from between feet all around the playground.

It was a bit consoling for Paul to realize that in their partnership that morning, one of them might dominate in one sort of activity, but the roles could be reversed in another. Without doubt Arthur had been the brains in the library, with Paul secretly feeling inferior, but just now Arthur was running round in circles like somebody's baby brother. Paul shouted advice and tried to keep the game away from Billy's sharp eyes, but there was no disguising from anyone the lowly level of what was going on – not even from the two girls off their table who strolled slowly past as if by chance.

'Brought your boots, Reet? I fancy our chances against this team!'

Paul, who was about to return a wide pass from Arthur with a showy back-flick, took his eyes off it to scorch a look at Lorraine, and missed it completely. He only just stopped himself falling over.

'Wouldn't be fair,' Rita giggled. 'Like taking sweets off a baby!'

The girls walked on, with several backward glances and a burst of private laughter exploding loud enough for the boys to hear. Clearly, Arthur couldn't have cared less as

54

he ran to get the missed ball back; but it got at Paul. Being giggled at by girls was something he'd never had to suffer before. Mouthing a curse at chance, Paul looked round at Billy again, moving to get a clear view. During the past ten minutes Paul had shot him the odd glance, checking that he was still in his goal and not starting some attack on them, but now all he wanted was to be dead sure Billy hadn't seen that terrible miss.

But there was no knowing, because he wasn't there. The game was still going on – someone else was in goal and all the rest were there – but there was no sign of Billy. What was he up to? Paul worried. He bet he hadn't just gone in to the lavatory. And for someone else to be in goal! His eyes narrowed with sharp purpose as he searched through three hundred and sixty degrees of windswept playground life, of earnest chasing faces, of matey grins, of gesticulating limbs. But he could catch no glimpse of Billy's red track-suit, no obvious sign of danger; just the relaxed sight of a couple of hundred children who, for the most part, were where they wanted to be.

'Well, who'd have thought I could do that?'

Arthur had got the ball back and now he dribbled it past Paul by running it over his left toe-cap and between his feet.

Paul hadn't time to congratulate him.

'Oh, well played Little Arthur!'

Lorraine and Rita were on their way back from where-ever they'd been.

'He's quite good,' said Rita. 'Compared with some . . .'

That was the final indignity for Paul. He had put up with being the secretary in the library, he had made a stupid mistake at football, he was playing out here with the one person he wouldn't normally choose – but he didn't have to take sarcasm from two stupid people like this. His plaguing frustration suddenly burst out, boiling, as the bell began to ring the end of the break.

'Clear off you two!' he shouted. 'Get lost!'

'Oh, charming!' Lorraine said sweetly, with a hint of a smile at getting some reaction. 'Didn't they teach you how to take a joke at your other school?'

'Get lost yourself!' added a hotter Rita. 'Come on, Lorr., it's "in" time.'

With a look which could almost have been taken for sympathy, Arthur handed the ball back to Paul.

'Let's go in,' he said, 'we can carry on with the card in the library; she said all morning if we liked . . .'

Paul agreed with a twist of his mouth and an anything-you-say lift of his eyebrows before suddenly putting his head down and running through the reluctant walkers into the school. It had become urgent, because as well as wanting to get well ahead of the loudly commenting girls, after his unfortunate display just now, which he had a horrible feeling had not gone unnoticed, he wanted the quiet privacy of the library even more than Arthur had wanted it earlier.

When he burst through its curtained door, however, hoping to shut it quickly behind him and lose himself in the map, he was pulled up with an audible catch of surprised breath by the sight of someone already there, leaning casually on a bookcase. It was Billy, of course. It had to be.

'Good in here, ain't it?' he said. 'In the library. Private.'

'I s'pose so.'

Paul didn't take his eyes off him. Now they were like two characters in the saloon again, one riling the other with polite talk, both aware to the millimetre how far their hands were from their gun-butts.

'Load of books, too.' Billy shifted his weight but showed no sign of going.

'Yeah . . .'

'Must be thousands of pages all told. Could be millions.'

'Could be.'

'Yes, millions, I'd say.'

Billy sauntered over to the door, while Paul turned to keep facing him all the while. Now for the exit line before he went. He'd come in here for something, and he was bound to be saving it to let it drop just as he went out. A parting shot. People like Billy were like that.

'Easy to lose a bit of writing paper in all those millions of pages . . .' His hand was on the yellow brass knob, ready.

'Could be . . .' So that was it. He needn't say any more.

'Definitely, I'd say.'

Then he was gone, flashing Paul a wide false smile and leaving the door wide open to show he wasn't scared of being followed. Paul rushed to the low circular table and shuffled the writing paper in a vain attempt to find what he knew wouldn't be there. Blast! His laborious scribbling had all gone for nothing; there were no notes left at all. Except one, in block capitals along the top of a clean sheet of paper. 'TONIGHT.'

For a hopeful half-minute Paul thought this dramatic scene and the loss of the notes might be some sort of payment in advance for a game over the park with Billy, something to show that he couldn't think he had earned it by his silence over the liquorice allsorts. Perhaps 'Tonight' meant something good, not bad. But his hopes fell back to a realistic level when Arthur came in and picked up the map, the first to spot it screwed-up on a book-shelf.

'What the devil have you done this for?' he demanded. 'That wasn't necessary, was it?' But before Paul could protest his innocence, or report the loss of the work-sheet,

Arthur went on, 'And she's going to be delighted with you, scribbling on it as well as screwing it up!'

Paul had to grab the map and twist it round his way to see what Arthur was going on about. But he didn't have to look hard to find it. Smack in the middle of the sheet, where the vertical line D met the horizontal line 4, there was a bold piratical cross. And immediately, Paul could see what it was meant to be: his rendezvous for the promised meeting with Billy. Now it all made sense: for the large pencil cross was scratched across the property on the corner of Orchard Road and Cherry Tree Way. And that was where Paul lived. That meant that Daineses' shop was where they'd meet after school – once again, it seemed, if Billy had his way.

Already confused by the big problem which now confronted him, Paul didn't know whether to be pleased or sorry when Arthur made light of the hiding of the paper. It was a relief when he didn't blow his top, but at the same time Paul couldn't see that his efforts before break were 'no great loss'. Arthur must have known Billy of old, Paul thought, for he made no other comment, just shrugged, when Paul told him what he'd done.

'The best course of action is for you to write down the answers we had before, and I'll look up this other name, Doran. We've got an hour so you can make it a fair copy as you go.' Arthur was very matter-of-fact.

Paul nodded. He was more like a teacher, this kid, dishing out his orders; and already he was a different person again from the boy who'd been making such a mess of kicking the ball in the playground. He sighed, and picked up his pencil. It was like he'd thought outside. One minute you were on top, the next minute you were underneath. Except with Billy. He couldn't see how he'd ever be on top with him.

What *did* the big dope think he was up to? All right, so

he didn't like Paul, didn't want him in his game, wasn't prepared to let him become part of anything worth joining. Well, perhaps that was because he didn't want to be challenged for the leadership of the gang; perhaps he thought he had to see Paul off. But why should that make him want to do this other thing to Paul; put him on the spot; make him choose between covering up for him in the shop and telling his dad? Perhaps that was just to rub it in, to make Paul realize for himself that he wouldn't tell, that Billy was boss. Or perhaps it was deeper than that! Perhaps this was all part of some elaborate trial or initiation test, and it would all end up with Paul, a proven loyalist, actually being welcomed into the group, under a cheerful battering of painful thumps on the back. Paul wasn't so sure about that; but he did know he didn't want another incident like the one in the shop the day before. He didn't want to have to choose again. He didn't want the responsibility of having to decide whether or not to tell his mum or his dad that Billy was working a fiddle. And why should he? Paul suddenly got angry when he thought of what might have been. Even without being one of the lads at school he had enjoyed being part of his parents' set-up at the shop for twenty minutes. At least they had come to realize that they needed him a bit; and he had been delighted at being able to help. And now Billy was ruining that for him as well.

Well, Billy wouldn't, he decided – breaking his pencil point with the force of his decision. No. He'd go back home the same as yesterday and serve in the shop, and if Billy came in he'd just keep whatever he wanted to buy on their side of the counter till Billy's money was safely in his hand. Billy couldn't twist them then unless he made a fuss – and then Paul's dad could sort it out. For a second Paul smiled. That'd be good. Really good. His dad sorting Richardson out! And he'd be damned careful, Paul told himself as an afterthought, to get one of his parents to check any change he had to give back to Billy. He wouldn't be caught like that. No, that was it. That's what he'd do. He'd be damned if he'd back down.

But Paul had finished writing only one more sentence before his resolve had gone again. He had that feeling he got waiting for a train, or going on holiday, except there was no pleasant destination at the end of this. He had a horrible premonition that something he couldn't control would happen. He tried to make himself angry again, to get back his confidence; but now it wasn't real, it was only surface, and he knew he was only acting it for himself. He made a faint little moaning sound. It was rotten the way your own feelings could change from minute to minute.

'Do you always talk to yourself when you're writing?'

'Eh? No. Was I?'

'Yes, mutter, mutter, mutter, groan, groan. And I can't find any mention of Doran anywhere.'

Paul pulled a face that he hoped conveyed regret; but that, too, felt horribly unnatural and false.

'But we won't let it beat us. We were doing quite well otherwise.'

'Yes.'

'I know, you come home with me after school and we'll do a bit of digging around. You can have some tea if you like. They won't mind . . .'

Paul looked at the other boy's face. Now it was friendly, hopeful, almost keen. So perhaps he wasn't a bad bloke, Arthur, underneath his bossy top surface. And he'd have a very reasonable excuse for dodging Billy in the shop if he accepted this invitation.

'You're not doing anything else special, are you?' Arthur was fixing him with his sharp green eyes, bringing the pressure of his own personality to bear on the new boy.

'No. Nothing special. I'll come.'

'Good. All right, carry on with your writing. And Paul . . .'

'Yeah?'

'No more muttering, eh?'

Chapter Seven

IT seemed ironic to be looking back to the unhappy day before with nostalgia, but that was the way Paul felt as he walked off with Arthur Little, away from the school and in the opposite direction to the shop. Yesterday afternoon he had hurried back to the shop to find a need to be there; today he was walking off the other way in spite of that same need. He had taken the easy way out, he knew that: he had accepted Arthur's friendly invitation to follow-up the morning's work back at the flats just so that he shouldn't have to confront Billy in the shop again. There was no kidding himself about his motive. And for that get-out he was leaving his mum and his dad in the lurch, and he was letting Arthur imagine their friendship was stronger than it really was. He was like a wind-blown seed, being spun about in the grey bluster, taking no de-cision, making no choice – except, perhaps, that of choos-ing not to choose.

'There it is, for what it's worth,' Arthur remarked as they turned to cross the awkward widening road by the junction. 'Doran House.'

Pleased to be distracted from his uncomfortable thoughts, Paul took a fresh look at the vaguely familiar three-storey block which sat opposite Victory Park; and suddenly he felt a bit sorry for Arthur. You either wanted to live in a proper house with a garden, he thought, or in a good high block of flats with lifts to play in and balconies to drop parachutes off; but this low barracks-like building seemed to have the worst aspects of both worlds: no gardens, and no height.

'Horrible, isn't it?' said the shrewd Arthur, reading Paul's thoughts from his face.

Together they looked at the façade: small windows separated by large areas of cracked brickwork, a widening green seepage from a faulty overflow, and stark black drainpipes branching out over its side like winter trees in a modern painting.

Arthur pointed to the tiled sign let into the wall. 'Doran House! Fancy being remembered by a place like this. Whoever he was.'

Paul stared at the name on the wall until it became a blurred and meaningless pattern of letters. *Doran.* No, it definitely didn't mean a thing.

'It's not tall enough for a lift, but we've got a do-it-yourself escalator,' Arthur said, and without bothering to turn for Paul's reaction he went on ahead up the hard stone stairs to the top floor.

The smells and the sounds of other people's lives mingled in the corridor as they filed along it – greens, disinfectant, toddlers, transistors, the living-together bit which Paul decided he wouldn't like – and only after Arthur had let them into the tiny hall with his door-key did Doran House strike Paul as providing any sort of home.

An old man stood rubbing his hands briskly in the doorway of the small bedroom off to the right of the hall. Paul looked up at the tanned face above the Fair Isle pullover.

'Hello,' Paul said, always a bit embarrassed at having to meet a new adult. It was the worst part of going to other boys' homes, he'd found, the adults; especially the grans and grandads who seemed to have so much time to talk to you.

'Hello, young man.'

There was something about the old boy that made Paul

feel extra uncomfortable, a bit nervous. He was so well turned-out, with such a firm voice and upright bearing – very different from some of the gummy old pards he'd known, like Simon Tulip's grandad who poked the fire with his boot and spat at pigeons.

'You're a new face, aren't you?' Arthur's grandad produced a shallow pipe with a silver rim. He rocked casually on to his toes to put Paul at his ease.

He was only trying to be helpful.

'Yes. My dad's bought Jobbers' shop . . .'

'Oh, I see. A bit like us. You're still a fish out of water for a bit? Not too many chaps to call your friends?'

'Yes.' He was dead right. Well, at least here was someone who understood what it was like. Paul relaxed a bit and looked at Arthur. But Arthur was pushing past, going on into the living-room as if Paul and the old man weren't there.

'You coming in, Paul? My mum'll say hello if you're quick.'

'Eh?'

'She's finishing an essay today, but she's trying to find her spare ball-point. It's a good time to disturb her.' It was all very matter-of-fact. 'Come on.'

'Tell her I'll lay on some tea in thirty minutes if she likes,' Arthur's grandfather said. 'I'll root around and find something she can eat while she's working.' He turned back to Paul. 'You'll have a spot to eat with us, won't you?'

'Yes, thanks.' That was different too. You usually got chased off home long before any food appeared, as if a father coming in for his dinner would run amok in the kitchen if he found you there.

'Jolly good. Until later, then.'

The old man shut his door quietly, and Paul found himself being steered by the arm into the living-room.

'Just say hello and we can go in my bedroom and decide what we're going to do.'

'O.K.' There was clearly no room for disagreement in Arthur's flat. Not by outsiders, anyway. They sounded like the sort of single-minded people who usually got their own way; so Paul obediently went where he was guided. In his time he had met many a boy's mother in the busyness of her own home. Such women had ranged from the prickly take-your-shoes-off-and-does-your-mother-know-where-you-are sorts who spoke from the depth of steamy kitchens, to the easy-going mums who made a big fuss of him and sent him on errands with their own sons to get last-minute things from the shops. But Paul decided he'd never been in a boy's home like this, where something other than the daily business of eating and cleaning, or eating and viewing, was of paramount importance.

'Come in, come in, come in. Why the hell do ball-points run out when you're in the middle of using them?'

The first view Paul had of Arthur's mother was of her jeaned bottom and half of her back over the arm of an elderly settee. But that hardly seemed unusual in the unexpectedness of that living-room.

'It's like dying, the way they give out in the middle of a sentence.' She was still upside-down and a bit muffled. 'You must invent one, Arthur, that changes colour or something about five hundred words before it gives up the ghost . . .'

The living-room was like Paul's idea of a newspaper office. There was paper on every available surface: sheets of lined exercise paper, loose paper, paper in students' pads; clean paper, and densely covered paper, with neat, square handwriting; there were scribblers, and files, and on the old-fashioned dining table piles of books with markers formed a barricade around the place where Mrs Little was doing her writing.

65

'Arthur tells me you're Paul. How do you do, Paul?'

Her voice was light and clear. She held out a slim smooth hand and shook Paul's with unexpected vigour. He thought she was very pretty. She had a red Indian hair-style with plaits and a headband, and round the neck of her cheesecloth shirt there were several chains and rows of beads. He couldn't help the disloyal thought that she looked years younger than his own mother, more like a big sister – and he'd always thought *she* looked something special at weddings and parties. To his intense discomfort he found himself going red for no reason.

With a gleam of triumph Arthur's mother suddenly held up a very expensive-looking stainless steel Parker. 'I thought so. I had this in my shoulder-bag.' She blew peppermint dust off it and clicked it once or twice. 'There we are, all ready to go again.'

She looked as pleased as Paul's mother did on birthday mornings. He smiled a willing interest in her pen problem, but before he could get further involved Arthur started to pull him out of the room.

'We're going in my bedroom,' he announced curtly.

Whether anything registered with her or not Paul couldn't be sure, but Mrs Little just carried on talking in the same fast intelligent-sounding way that she had since they had come in.

'So we've solved the writing problem. Good. Nice to have met you, Paul. See you again . . .'

'Yes you will, he's staying for tea . . .'

If she heard the news it was found unworthy of comment. 'Have you seen that small book of poems with red wine stains on the cover?'

'Nope.'

She was off pursuing her own thoughts again, but Arthur obviously wasn't going to be side-tracked either. Within ten seconds Paul was in his bedroom, his final view of Mrs Little the same as his first as she dipped under the table among a toppled pile of paperbacks.

'Now,' said Arthur, 'this Doran business . . .'

Paul sat on Arthur's bed and waited for the next assault on his open mind. He'd never met anything like this family, all self-contained in their separate rooms. His own experience, before the shop, had been of through-lounges, wide hatches into kitchens, open-plan lay-outs, everybody in together – usually watching television. Here everybody wanted elbow-room to do their own thing. And this room, looking like a miniature military academy, dramatically showed what Arthur needed room for. The walls were filled with the deep reds and blues of museum posters of military uniforms, a large painted model of a trooper stood on the top of his book-case, and, spread out on a low wide coffee table under the window, like a view from the hill, were two scaled-down model armies lined up in battle formations. Field Marshall Little, you could call him, Paul thought.

Arthur saw Paul's eyes lingering there.

'This isn't a real battle,' he explained enthusiastically, 'it's not a reconstruction of anything that really happened. This army here,' he indicated the rows of grey, green and blue troops with his long fingers, 'these have all been given to me by different people; a mixture of troops from different times. But these here,' his left hand circled in the air above the neat ranks of red, possessively, 'Wellington's infantry, these are all my men.' He laughed, seriously. 'I've got them lined up to fight the battle of Doran Heights!'

Paul, his interest very much awakened, knelt down on the floor by the table. He'd seen a programme about people – grown-ups – who fought long, thought-out battles with model soldiers, but he'd never realized they were like this. The models were so small. They put him in mind of his Subbuteo team of miniature footballers in their size and their detail.

'Play against yourself, do you?'

'Yes, mostly. The old man plays now and again, but he won't remember the rules.'

'Like Subbuteo, this is. I play against myself, reds v. whites. But there's not so many men to move about as here ...' Paul bent down on a level with the table, impressing himself with his defender's view of an attacking column. Down here they looked very real, if you didn't peer too closely at their expressionless faces. 'How do you know when you've won? Fire matchsticks and see how many you can knock over?'

'What? No!' Arthur's laugh embraced surprise and pity in its false humour. 'It's all tactics. Strategy. It's all dependent on what artillery you bring, how you've deployed your men, just like in real life ...'

'Oh.' Subbuteo was simpler, Paul thought. You just scored goals in that; although the way you used your men made some difference. 'Yes,' he drew out slowly, just to keep himself crouching there a little longer. This was really something. He wouldn't mind being asked to play a game of this.

'Now, Doran.' Arthur was kneeling on his bed looking in an old encyclopedia on the shelf.

Oh. So Paul wasn't going to be invited to a game. The same old story, this week. He stood up reluctantly, unwilling to drag his eyes away from the battlefield. Already he could see a useful move he'd make with the hotch-potch army.

'Nothing here.'

'What, no Doran?' His interest sounded so false to himself that he wondered Arthur didn't make some sarcastic remark. He was only putting it on now. If he were honest he'd say he couldn't have cared less if the flats were called

'Arthur Little House'. He had come here on a soft option, to avoid Billy Richardson in the shop, and now he was having to pay for it with a bit of pretended interest.

'No, not a hint of anything.' Arthur closed the encyclopedia and put it back on the shelf, being careful to position it in its right place among the other numbered volumes. 'It must be local, then, a public benefactor of some sort, or a landowner, perhaps . . .'

'Could be.' That was good news. That meant they'd just have to ask someone, and Paul wouldn't be spending hours copying chunks out of a book. 'We'll just have to ask someone, then. Like your grandad. He might know. Go ̄ ask him.' The sooner this was over with and they could play a game with the soldiers the better.

But Arthur was wrinkling up his nose. 'I don't know. That seems too easy somehow. It's not the same as knowing, or finding out for ourselves, if we ask. It's like getting someone to do homework for you. It's not like being a researcher . . .' His eyes flickered in the direction of the living-room, where his mother was working.

Paul didn't agree. 'Well, if it comes out of a book someone's telling you, aren't they? And if you ask someone, someone's telling you. Someone's telling you both ways. So if you can find the answer quickly by asking someone, then you ought to ask them.'

Arthur's nose wrinkled again. Already Paul was beginning to dislike that look. Arthur did it a lot, come to think of it. A quick tap on the end of that nose would soon knock the wrinkle off it, he thought.

'I'm not sure. I suppose it's all right if they've got something to do with what you're researching – I mean, as long as you're not giving in by asking . . .'

The look had gone, and Paul, suddenly ashamed, unclenched the pretended fist behind his back.

'Yes, 'course. I just thought it didn't make a difference either way . . .'

But Arthur was moving on already. 'My mother's busy so we'll ask the old man. Perhaps if he just gives us a hint to put us on the right track . . . But don't expect too much. The only things old soldiers seem able to remember are the names of old battles.'

Of course! Paul might have known. Now he thought about it, the old boy had soldier written all over him. The erect stance, the clear voice, the confident tone, the attempts to put you at your ease. And definitely an officer, a commander.

'Was he famous? A hero, in the war?'

'The first. He was too old for the second, our Major West.'

Arthur seemed very off-hand about it, Paul thought; but he nodded, waiting to be told more. There wasn't any.

'Let's go and ask him about Doran, and then get him to get the tea. I'm hungry . . .'

That didn't seem to be any way to treat a famous old soldier, Paul thought; but he obediently followed Arthur across the narrow passage to the closed door. He waited for the polite knock, and the word of command to go in. But without ceremony Arthur opened the door and walked straight into the small room. Paul half expected to see a disturbed face turning angrily from a deep armchair, the mouth open ready to rebuke them for walking straight in while he was reading. But the old man was not reading in a deep armchair; he was on the bed, sound asleep, lying there neatly with his mouth wide open and his breath exchanging places with the atmosphere in a series of deep, throaty, groans.

'Oh God, he's playing Rip Van Winkle again!'

It was a rare shaft of humour from Arthur; perhaps a family joke; and Paul's genuine laugh lifted the curtain on the old man's consciousness. He turned his head towards them, his eyes glazed with drowsiness, looking but failing to see for a few seconds. Paul expected sudden movement next, a snapping-to, before the retired soldier spoke; but there was none. The stare continued, coma-like, so that his words when they came were something of a surprise attack.

'Arthur, my lad, a few years back I'd have had anyone's guts for garters who did that to me!'

There was enough of a hard edge on the voice for Paul to guess that it was probably true, and he took the smallest step back.

'It's too early to be asleep, lazybones. You'll be wandering around all night. And we haven't had our tea yet.'

Good God! Arthur really was asking for a thick ear! Paul imagined talking to Grandad Daines like that. There'd be a long hurt silence, and then a solemn sermon about manners – probably followed by a bony clout.

'Come on, then, spit it out. What d'you want?' He swung his legs off the bed and sat up quickly, the movement typical of someone years younger.

'Doran House,' said Arthur, unruffled. 'This place, the name Doran. Does it mean anything to you? We just want a small clue ...'

The old man wiped his full nose with his handkerchief, finishing with an impatient to-and-fro movement. 'Now let me see. Doran ...' He looked intently at his feet, and the room waited as if expecting a tactical decision from the commanding officer. 'I knew a Doran out in India, but he was just a champion pig-sticker; military police-man type; hardly a character anyone would name a block of flats after ... No, I can't help you with this place.' He suddenly laughed, a young chuckle. 'But I can show you a picture of the other one!'

'Oh, no! Not your photographs! A fate worse than

death!' Arthur moaned. 'He's come to tea, not to be bored rigid!'

'Please yourself, then. But he can see them sometime, if he likes.' The old man looked at Paul. 'I've got them all up there, you know.' He indicated the top of the tall old-fashioned wardrobe with his hand. 'I was a war photographer you know, rank of Major; and some people have found my stuff interesting. They always said I could tell a better story with six photographs than some chaps could with six thousand words . . .'

Was it nervous excitement that had suddenly turned Paul's stomach over, or the guilty thought of wardrobe tops and the secretly growing mound of litter on the top of his own? Perhaps it was both; it was hard to tell. The old man looked at Arthur, although they both guessed he couldn't win. What Arthur said, went. But Paul couldn't help wishing he could get a look at some of the Major's war pictures.

'How about it, then?'

'Yes, please,' Paul nodded. 'Yes.'

'Splendid. Well, I'll get them down.' Major West suddenly shook Paul's hand as if they'd come to a gentleman's agreement. 'Tomorrow night, eh? Never any sense in hanging fire, is there?'

'No. Yes, please.' Paul agreed quickly and mentally decided to make it convenient later, if need be. There was no saying no to people like Arthur and his grandfather. And besides, he wanted to come and see them.

'And we can round it off with something special to eat, eh?'

'Yes, please.'

'I've got one or two juicy pork chops in the top of the refrigerator. I'll thaw them out, cook them gently, and serve them with a bottle of something special . . .'

'Mmmmm.' Paul nodded vigorously. He hadn't eaten

yet, and the thought of a pork chop suddenly awakened a physical need.

'Splendid.'

'Well what about tea tonight?' Arthur suddenly demanded. 'I'm starving. And what about Doran?'

The Major slowly got up off the bed. 'Tea is coming, sir,' he said, standing to attention, and scorning to lean on old age as a reason for being addressed politely. 'But Doran, *your* Doran, is beyond my capability.'

'Oh. Thanks for nothing.'

Paul, again feeling uncomfortable at Arthur's tone, and not wanting to see a distinguished soldier having to get cross with him, tried to steer the conversation on to a safe course.

'We'll just have to give in and ask Miss,' he said.

The reply he got shook him.

'No!'

It was firm and it was clear. But it wasn't what was said that floored him. It was the fact that both Arthur *and* his grandfather had said it, with one voice.

Paul tightened his mouth into a thin line and left the matter there. It wasn't so much that he minded being disagreed with: what he didn't like was being shown by such a spontaneous demonstration that, whatever slight warmth had seemed to develop in the past few minutes between himself and the Major, however the old man and Arthur might have rubbed each other up the wrong way, when it came to a matter of principle, Paul could still be the odd man out.

Chapter Eight

PAUL was half-way home before it struck him. After a plate of banana sandwiches and a cup of coffee, he had said he had to go, and had gone. And he had got two hundred metres down the road before he realized that for the past two hours he'd not given a single thought to Billy Richardson. He'd forgotten him to the extent of not even keeping a weather-eye open for him on the street. Not only that, he thought, his conscience catching up with him as if it were on elastic, he'd forgotten all about his parents and their need to have him in the shop after school. Oh God! His high spirits drooped. Having let them down in order to avoid Billy, the time had come to pay up; he'd got to face them now. With a suddenly renewed dislike for Billy — and hoping like mad that he wouldn't bump into him after all that — Paul ran fast towards home. He might as well get the unpleasantness over and done with as quickly as possible.

There were still lots of kids about. There was a little boy, grimy-faced and runny-nosed, wailing on the pavement outside his house where someone had shut the gate on him; two big kids circled round and round a lamp-post on old bikes, trying to force each other to make a mistake and come crashing off; and there were the late summer sounds of children in their gardens and over in Victoria Park beyond — shrill voices, broken voices, laughing and quarrelling voices. Everything seemed so normal as far as everyone else was concerned. But for Paul it was yet another moment of anxiety as he ran back towards the shop.

With some relief, having neither seen nor heard Billy Richardson, Paul quietly let himself in through the side door of the closed shop. He didn't want to announce his late arrival with too much of a flourish. At the old house he'd been well used to a good ticking-off for all sorts of misdeeds, but since they'd been here there hadn't been the cause, he'd been treated like someone older. In a strange way it was one of the things he missed. At least it showed you were being noticed if people had a go at you now and again. Like the old Major in putting up with Arthur. It was better than being ignored. But just now, though, he thought the quiet life would suit him better. Cautiously, he put his head round the door of the kitchen, and then the living-room. They were both empty. For a third time he assumed his big-eyed and innocent face and gently opened the door into the shop.

'Thanks a bundle!' It was his father. 'A great time to let us down!'

A block of icy anticipation froze Paul's stomach as he turned his face to a silent look of apology before withdrawing a few centimetres. But when he heard a kick and the thump of his father's hand on the freezer he boldly took a step further into the shop.

'That won't cure anything!' his mother shouted. 'I've taken a fuse out of the iron. I'll try that. You mop up that water before it soaks into the floor. For God's sake pull yourself together and do something useful instead of ranting and raving at the blessed thing!'

Paul walked round the counter to where his parents were kneeling red-faced before the large grocery deep-freeze, his father starting to dab half-heartedly at a small pool of water beneath the silent machine, his mother fiddling with a greasy plug she'd pulled from a socket in the darkness behind it.

'It couldn't pack up when we were as near empty as

dammit, sweating on that bloody delivery! No, it has to wait till we're crammed full with a few hundred quid's worth of stock before it pulls this little trick! You can't re-freeze this, you know. Once it's thawed it's dead . . .'

'And if the worst comes to the worst we claim it on the insurance. It's not the end of the world. Come on, hurry up, I want to plug it in again . . .'

Mrs Daines looked up and saw Paul, but she said nothing. A fleeting squeeze of her eyes acknowledged his presence, but she was too busy groping in an awkward position for the dusty socket to say anything.

Five minutes later a flicker on the television screen and a sudden squeaking chug from the shop told Paul that she had succeeded. The deep-freeze panic was over. His own absence, if it had been noticed, was secondary to the elec-trical problem. If it was going to be mentioned at all now – and he very much doubted if it was – it would have a pretty low priority.

He finished the Mars bar he'd just taken and stuffed the paper in his pocket. He felt a little better. Having something to eat was like having a bit of company, he decided. Just for a few minutes, while it lasted. Perhaps if things were different, if he felt more settled here, it wouldn't be necessary. And then it would be time to get his wardrobe top cleared! He dismissed the thought and turned his attention back to the *Midweek Movie*, and he suddenly wondered if Simon Tulip was watching it up in London . . .

Paul was in two minds about taking his football to school the next day. By not taking it he wouldn't be em-barrassed by having to play passing-the-ball with Arthur at break-time; on the other hand that might look to Billy as if he had given up hope of ever playing football at all. And he didn't want to have to stay in the library all day, or mooch around the playground avoiding the teasing remarks of Lorraine and Rita. So in the hope that there might be some third choice open to him – he didn't know what – he took it, buried deep in a plastic bag beneath his P.E. things.

To make things as smooth for himself as possible he used a strategy as deliberately as Arthur might in a war game. He walked to school slowly, checking with his watch every now and then, and he timed his arrival to coincide with the 'in' whistle: so he made sure he didn't have to make any decisions about what to do before school. In fact, he was through the classroom door and heading for his seat that morning before anyone could even speak to him.

'What you got there?'

Oh no! After all that! His spirits sank with the thought of having been outmanoeuvred. The voice came from behind him, from someone waiting behind the classroom door. He didn't need to turn round to know who. There was no mistaking that aggressive tone.

'Got your ball, 'ave you?'

'Yeah,' he said. But that was the only word; Paul's clear defiant meaning was, *So what*?

'Good. Some twit punctured our'n on a rose bush. It's not the 'eavy one?'

'No.'

'Right. See you behind the kitchen, our place, sharp on the buzzer. Right?'

Paul stared at the seated Arthur, who was seemingly engrossed in a book, as he gave an immediate reply. 'Yeah, if you like.' Like last night, with the old man's invitation, he'd agree first and worry about making it right later.

Worry? Why worry? He suddenly snapped-to. Wasn't this what he'd wanted all along? Hadn't he been trying for two days to get in with a crowd, become part of a game, of a gang, like Simon Tulip's? Well, now it looked

77

as if he'd made it. Where was the worry about that? This must mean he'd passed whatever stupid test Billy had been mucking about giving him in the past couple of days, and now the kids wanted him in. All right, so they were making an excuse about it being his football they were after; but you had to let people have an excuse. No, there was no worry, definitely. The only slight complication was Arthur, but he didn't owe Arthur anything, did he? Neither of them owned the other. Paul suddenly began to feel quite light-hearted. He turned round to grin at Billy, but he wasn't quite quick enough and the boy passed him on his other side, flipping Arthur's book closed as he sauntered by to his table. Paul's spirits dropped again. There was no need for that, he thought: that didn't help him with Arthur: after all, they'd had a common enemy in Billy when he'd tried to spoil their work the day before, and it could look a bit like changing sides if Billy was rotten to Arthur.

Again Paul was reluctant to be the first to speak, and Arthur seemed to be engrossed in finding his place, so it was left to Lorraine to fill the silence on the table.

'Oh, hello,' she said to Paul. 'Where was you last night? I came in your shop for a Cadbury's Flake and your mum had to see to me. She's nice, your mum . . .'

Paul had to stop himself from replying too quickly. But it was urgent. Never mind his mum at this moment; he didn't want her spreading it round that he'd been up at Arthur's, not now that he'd had an invitation to play football with the boys at break-time. Billy would make a right meal of that. Arthur's sudden stillness told Paul he was listening for the way he would reply to the nosy girl, but he felt he had to put his own interests first. He'd got more to lose here than the self-contained Arthur had.

'I was out,' he replied, as nonchalantly as he could.

'Up Arthur's wasn't you?'

'Eh?' Paul could see Arthur downright staring at him now. 'Oh, yes, for a bit ...' He threw up his desk-lid and fumbled for something, anything, inside. How the hell did she know where he'd been? And what was the point of asking him, then, unless she just wanted to show him up? He looked at his simple reading book, one he'd read before at the other school when he'd been younger; and suddenly he couldn't help but think how nice and uncomplicated life had been when he was seven.

Paul could almost feel Arthur's green eyes sending their laser beams through the desk-lid, and he could sense Lorraine's off-hand teasing face waiting with the next gibe to get him going as soon as he lowered it. But he couldn't stay in there for ever.

Lorraine didn't wait. She was always a jump ahead, leapfrogging the comment you were prepared for. 'Oh, can't you find it, Paul?' she said with exaggerated concern. 'D'you want any help?' she poked a smiling, curly, head over his desk top.

'No thanks,' he muttered gruffly. There was that funny feeling again, like in the old man's bedroom when the talk had been of the photographs on the wardrobe top: that same mixed-up ache that didn't know whether it was pleasure or guilt. But Paul's brain analysed it for him. It was guilt, and he felt bad. It surely couldn't be pleasure, just because some stupid girl wouldn't leave him alone, could it?

Miss Simmonds, without knowing it, saved Paul from further embarrassment. She started to call the register, and immediately after assembly she announced a maths test to see what the class could do. So luckily there was no question of his being on his own in the library with Arthur, puzzling over place-names and being forced to apologize for his erratic behaviour. And Paul knew he had time during the whole of the rest of the day to swing it so that he still went home to Arthur's to see the photographs, so at least for a while he was able to concentrate on the work he'd been set.

He knew it was best not to get bogged down in explanations about Billy to Arthur. He would just go out to play, and if Arthur wanted to follow and take his chances in getting a game like any normal boy that was up to him. It was no more than he had had to do on the first day of term, Paul told himself.

As it happened the ball was pattering along the surface of the playground at Paul's feet before Arthur finished reading and tidied his book away; but Paul still couldn't wait to get round the corner by the kitchens, out of sight of the main stretch of playground.

' 'Ere y'are mate, over 'ere !'

Someone on Paul's left was calling for the ball, and a sudden thrill of pleasure at the sound of it shivered down his spine and wrapped itself round his waist as if he were being hugged from behind. He found himself actually having to overcome a weakening of the muscles down the fronts of his thighs as he prepared to side-foot the ball to the boy he could see on the edge of his vision. *This* was what he'd been longing for. *This* was what it was all about. It was no wonder he felt nervous about making it good.

He was pleased with his first pass, and he hoped there were others running out behind him to see it. He'd put it a metre or so in front of the other boy and sprinted on for the expected return. But it didn't come. Instead, the boy, who was about Paul's height and with a brush of overgrown cropped hair, turned and put the ball back to Billy, who was trotting out like an international on the long run from Wembley's tunnel to the far goal. Billy flicked it up into his arms and bounced it, testing it, the rest of the way into his goal. Paul stopped running and stood still. Obviously nothing started without Billy's say-so.

There were six of them in the game: three, with Billy, kicking out, and three, including Paul, kicking in. No one asked Paul what position he normally played or whether he was right or left footed. It was just, 'You and you, back four, and you three, strikers.' And the game began with a high punt out.

Paul positioned himself over the far right, where he could use his better foot to send centres across without the responsibility of having to score. It would do for a start. He could turn on a bit of scoring skill later. The brush-headed boy, Mark, was against him, while a tall curly kid, all elbows, defended on the right. Paul took careful note of his own side. The boy who had chosen to go in the middle – the one Paul would want to oust before the whistle went – was short and stocky and ran up to the ball each time as if he were going to kick it with both feet at once; but his style belied a solid efficiency, a bustling striker who clearly got results. The other attacker, over on the left, was a scrawny blond kid in Wellington boots; but he seemed at home in them and he didn't appear to be at all handicapped by their soft awkwardness. But it was Billy who was the focus of Paul's attention, the unpredictable boy who'd tricked him, threatened him, and now allowed him into the privileged game. And yet to look at him in the goal he seemed just an ordinary kid, nothing special.

You got plenty of the ball, Paul found, if you hung back deep where Billy's big clearance went. When it was kicked out high it only meant someone turning and running after it every time, whereas if you were lurking there you got a fair run at the ball and the chance to set up a good move. After a reasonable start, with plenty of the ball and a few fair passes – some intentional, some lucky –

Paul began to feel he had a chance of showing this lot that they'd got a find here.

"'Ere, mate, on me 'ead!'

Paul pushed the ball ahead of him, being sure not to let it run too near the boy with the hair, and he looked up to see where Wellington boots was. He'd shouted for it, he could have it, right where he wanted it, on his head. Paul leaned his body back so as to lift the ball and he caught it nicely with his right instep. It was flighted well, and it made Paul feel good as he ran on in to see the boy in the middle head it towards the goal. He didn't score. Billy caught it expertly and without too much trouble; but that wasn't important to Paul. What mattered was the low grunt of 'good ball' from the stocky attacker as he turned and ran out again. Billy was too bound up with his own handling of the ball to say anything; but praise from any one of them would do to be going on with.

It suddenly began to feel like Sunday morning. It was a good moment, and there was the promise of more to come.

The ball went out to the left, and with the central attacker running out it seemed sensible for Paul to run into the vacant space in front of the goal on the chance of a nod-on himself. He ran on in. This was where he really wanted to be, close enough to contest the ball with Billy.

He looked again at the boy, skipping about in front of the wall, his mind totally involved for the moment with the bounce of the ball. He seemed to be two people, Billy. At the moment he was a goalkeeper, setting out to prove in every move he made that he was good – the best – and with his mouth kept unusually shut you wouldn't know he wasn't a decent kid. But at the end of the game he would no doubt go back to being that strange, threatening, antisocial character who seemed to take so much pleasure in being unpleasant. Why? Paul wondered. What made

Billy act the way he did? It didn't seem to make any sense.

A few words he might use began to run through Paul's head, something friendly to say to Billy as they stood close together waiting for the return of the ball. 'You're quite useful, mate. Always play in goal, do you?' Something like that. Something to establish contact between them. But he never got round to saying them. For a start, one of the others was near enough to hear, and he didn't want anyone to think he was crawling. And then the ball came over and he suddenly had a chance to do rather than say; physical rather than verbal contact.

The boy on the left centred the ball, his Wellingtons lifting it high, just the sort of centre a goalkeeper and a centre-forward would have to contest; and before either Billy or Paul had time to think about it the ball was dipping towards them and they were both moving forward and jumping.

Paul had taken-off fractionally before Billy in a bid to outjump him, and his head met the falling ball a split second before Billy's reaching fingertips, arching it in a high lob over Billy to bounce cleanly against the wall in the centre of the goal.

Paul didn't see it land. He had known it was a goal as soon as his head had met it, but Billy, coming down, landed hard across his neck and shoulder and the next second they were both off their feet in a heap on the tarmac, each flattened on the hard and gritty surface by the sprawling limbs of the other.

The elation Paul felt was hard to define. It was probably the goal that made his stomach tingle with a warm pleasure, for even in a pick-up game in the play-ground a goal is a goal; but it could have been the boy's silence after the hardness of the knock, the mutual acceptance of the tumble, the strange feeling of sharing an experience which a sporting tussle brings.

The goalkeeper picked himself up and gave Paul the space to get to his feet too.

'Good goal, mate!' someone said behind him. 'Unlucky Billy, nice attempt . . .'

Paul still waited for Billy's reaction. He'd said nothing so far. From past experience Paul could have expected him to sullenly demand a free kick for a foul. Or just claim that it had missed. But he said nothing. He kicked the ball out and restarted the game, and Paul wasn't to notice until later the grazes on their knees.

When the whistle went and the small group walked towards the school Paul made sure to walk well away from Billy, not because he didn't want to be associated with the other boy, but, on the contrary, because he wanted nothing to damage the delicate tendrils of a relationship which the game had begun to grow between them. Paul saw nobody else. He passed Arthur, standing in the windy sun and thinking his secret thoughts, and he passed Rita and Lorraine, making inaudible comments for his benefit. He saw and heard no one in that heightened state of pleasure at having been accepted into Billy's game, at having scored a goal, and at having fairly flattened by the boy. As he clutched his red football he was as aware of Billy's distance behind him as a pilot is of another plane in the sky, and there was only one pair of footsteps in the playground, and one voice in the whole school.

It spoke.

' 'Ere, son. 'Ow about after school, over the park, for a game?'

Paul's reply was as swift and as regardless as any he had given that week.

'O.K.,' he said.

That Arthur had heard both the question and the reply was of as little consequence at that moment as Rita's

84

remark to Lorraine. ' 'Ere, Lorr., look who's in with the big boys!'

And no one but Lorraine knew that she frowned when she heard it.

Paul could have spent the rest of the day worrying about Arthur, once he had decided to play football with Billy instead of going back to the flats after school: but it didn't occur to Paul to take Arthur's feelings into account; and not without reason, Paul thought. It was Arthur himself. If he had talked about the evening ahead, looked forward in some way to the special meal and the Major's photographs, then Paul might have had a tussle with his conscience; but Arthur just withdrew into his reading book and he gave Paul no reason for making a difficult decision. And then there was Mr Griffiths. As Paul walked into school from the playground, clutching his plastic football and followed by Billy and the others – silent now for some good reason of their own – the headmaster made the optimistic remark that he was glad Paul had made some friends so quickly. And how right he was, when you weighed it up, Paul thought. After all, he had only been at the school for two days and a bit, and he was in the thick of it. The fortnight's loneliness before term couldn't really count. And if the headmaster was pleased he was in with Billy, well, there seemed no reason at all to worry about Arthur. You couldn't please everyone.

It was a happy day for Paul. Since the shouts of the team on Sunday had told him what he was missing he had yearned for a moment like this, trooping in with the lads, and with a place in the school team as good as earned. He deserved it, he felt, and no quiet voice was going to interfere inside his head to tell him what he ought to feel about Arthur.

Paul played football with the same small crowd again at dinner time and at break-time in the afternoon, but there was no more goal-scoring drama. All that didn't seem to matter, though. He only had to think back to that tussle with Billy, and forward to the game in the park, to dispel before they formed any awkward thoughts he might have about Arthur or the old man.

Even so, the final buzzer found Paul meticulously tidying his half-empty desk. As the end of the afternoon had approached he had timed his final movements and his disappearance into his desk by the classroom clock, and he was able to keep his head down and avoid seeing Arthur lingering for a moment behind his upturned chair. He saw his feet, the old-fashioned black shoes, the narrow frayed bottoms of the thin jeans, and for a second – just a second – he was torn between feeling sorry for the boy and angry with him for hovering there. But at last the feet had moved away and Paul felt free to curl round and look over his left shoulder towards Billy's noisy corner of the classroom. And what he saw made him feel glad he'd seen Arthur off. This was more like old times with Simon Tulip.

Now that the class had been dismissed Trevor Dalton could moan out loud for the first time about his lost Wellington. Billy, or someone near him, had whipped it away when he had eased his hot foot out to have a scratch, and for the past fifteen minutes he'd been going quietly mad. But now Miss Simmonds was gone Dalton was free to have a loud go at the others.

'Come on, who's got it, then?'

Paul straightened up and smiled. They might as well know he liked a bit of fun, a muck-about too.

'I said where's me boot? Me foot's cold!'

'Oh, leave it out, Dalton,' Billy said, with a fine display of pretended innocence. 'I don't know, do I? 'Ave you lost it then?'

'No, I always go round hopping on one leg!'

'There's a funny old smell in 'ere,' said Mark with the brush hair, hardly able to get the words out through his wide wet grin. 'A right niff . . .'

'Yeah, rough, that smell. Is it your feet, Dalton?'

'You . . .'

'No, it's not 'is *feet*,' Billy corrected. '*Foot*. It's 'is *foot*. That bare one without the welly. The other one's all right . . .'

'You . . .' But Trevor Dalton wouldn't say more to Billy. He just made a general exasperated noise. He knew he'd get his boot back in Billy's own good time. Meanwhile, the laughing got to the slightly forced, cackling stage.

'Come on, then,' said Billy. 'Can't 'ang about here all day in this pong . . .' He got up and led the noisy gang towards the classroom door, banging into desks and toppling chairs.

Paul, still grinning and fully expecting the morning's invitation to be renewed, stood up and waited. It was a pity he couldn't sit a bit nearer to these lads, he thought, if he was going to be one of the gang. You couldn't share things properly if you were on the other side of the room.

But Billy didn't speak to Paul. He walked straight past Paul as if he were the Invisible Man. Fighting a look of disappointment off his face, Paul watched the others go by, Trevor Dalton coming last and making hard work of hopping between the desks. Billy and the gang clustered at the classroom door, and with an air of expectancy they waited for the boy with one boot to come a little nearer.

'Come on, you swines, who's got it?'

Everyone but Trevor Dalton was standing still and Paul, puzzled, disappointed, frustrated, and wondering in a flash of guilt how far Arthur would have got by then, turned back to his desk to close the lid.

But it was impossible to do it. Dalton's lost Wellington

was lying there like a dead limb, preventing the lid from closing properly. Who the hell had put that there? And when? Paul turned back to face the yelps of laughter coming from the boys by the door just as Trevor Dalton elbowed him aside and grabbed his property.

'Want duffin', do you?' he asked, holding the boot like a flexible club, and only a fraction off using it. There were obviously those who were allowed to tease Trevor Dalton, and those who weren't.

Paul flashed back. 'Any time you wanna try!' It was bravado, but now wasn't the time to be outdone in verbal threats.

'Oh, come on,' said Billy, 'let's get over the park and bags the goal.' And he led the way out of the room. The others followed him, including Dalton, who was hopping and crouching to put on his boot. Paul had obviously seen him off all right. But the big question was, did Billy still mean Paul to play? Had this all been just another of his funny tricks? Perhaps he couldn't help behaving like this, like a sort of Jekyll and Hyde. Paul didn't know; he was totally mixed up; he'd never come across a kid as hard to understand as Billy. But just as that depressing puzzlement was beginning to give way to a feeling of self-pity at missing out all round, the vacant look of the cupboard top became obvious to him. His plastic bag with the ball wasn't there any more.

Thank God for that! A pang of the morning's pleasure came back to cheer him. Of course. Billy had taken it. He'd taken it for the game over the park. And that could only mean one thing: like Trevor Dalton with his boot, Paul was meant to follow to get it.

Chapter Nine

NOBODY made any bones about Paul's arrival on the pitch. He hadn't felt confident enough to catch up with the group walking ahead of him, but, instead, he walked along about thirty metres behind, just giving them time to claim the near goal and start kicking about with his ball before he walked round the posts with his hands in his pockets to join them.

Although it was still early in the season the goal-mouth had that bald baked look of over-use. Already the dry cracks were opening up, and the pebbles dislodged themselves easily from their smooth sockets just below the surface. It contrasted strongly with the goal-mouths in the London parks Paul was used to. If a crowd of boys kicked about in a goal-mouth on a week-day there, they'd soon be sent packing by some bossy park-keeper. Goal-mouths had to be protected. But when you looked at the neglected ground here you could see the sense in it, Paul thought.

No one looked at him especially. Why should they? They weren't all bound up with Paul Daines and his problems of settling in. Each of them had his own life to lead, his own set of hurdles to jump. It was only Billy and Paul who had seemed to be running towards the same hurdle from opposite directions.

Somehow, by accident or design, Billy kicked a high ball out which was well over to the right towards Paul. Paul's hands were out of his pockets instantly, and all his skills of body balance and control went into his attempt to return it accurately into the centre, low this time, for someone to run on to and volley in.

It was the start of a marvellous game in which Paul became completely immersed. It was the other Billy in goal again: tall, athletic, totally immersed as well, and, as he'd been that morning, less argumentative and petulant than Paul had seen him previously. Perhaps it was because he was playing well. There was no knowing. The others played well, too. Trevor Dalton's temporary loss of a Wellington boot might never have happened – he called for the ball, he passed it, and when the sides changed he tackled and tussled, all without acrimony, and the group of boys went on playing harmoniously until the gathering darkness began to soften the edges of the buildings against the low sky, and the early lights came on one by one in the houses and in the darkening wedge of Doran House. Paul saw the first yellow oblong to signal the beginning of the evening for someone in the flats, but there was only the briefest glimmer of a thought about Arthur and the old man. It was Paul's header now which mattered, not what he might have been doing; and after the header, it was the next free kick, and then the next tackle.

Darkness was coming between them with the tangibility of a black fog when a loud spiral of stomach rumble told Paul that he was hungry. Mark, the boy with the spiky hair, suddenly decided that he had better get his tea before a clout from his mother ruined his appetite, and when he had gone and the balance of the game had been upset, Billy took the decision that they were all ready for something to eat.

'. . . and the final whistle goes!' he called, his voice rising to a crescendo as he kicked the ball high into the air. 'This man Richardson goes off to the cheers of the crowd . . .'

Paul ran to retrieve his ball. It had been a good evening, a good day, all told. He caught the others up and tucked himself into the group to join in the general talk about the game. Great, this was, just like at the other school with Simon Tulip and the gang; but now he felt too content even to compare this moment with any other. That had been then, and this was now, and this was what was important. And in his happy state he accepted Billy's arm round his shoulder as being perfectly natural, not a bit remarkable under the circumstances. It was warm, friendly, and like their earlier collision the contact seemed to link them together in a way which words couldn't. Just a few more steps, and Paul would raise the question of school football, when the first match was, what colours they played in, and all that. But just now Billy was talking about food.

'You know what I fancy?' he mused aloud. 'A nice plate of scampi and chips.'

They were all quiet for a few seconds, each of them picturing the popular take-away meal in the white-polystyrene tray from Toni at the fish and chip shop.

'Yeah,' said Trevor Dalton, 'be all right, but you'll get beans on toast same as me an' like it . . .'

Billy wasn't to be put down, though, not even in his imaginings. 'Scampi and chips,' he repeated, his weight on Paul, his hand dangling limply over his chest, 'followed by Arctic Roll . . .'

'Yeah, Arctic Roll; I like Arctic Roll.' Paul was happy to agree.

'In a proper caff, a proper meal like on the telly,' Billy enlarged as they all turned left out of the park gates, Trevor Dalton walking in the gutter to keep the line-abreast, 'with a Shandy an' a box of After Eights to finish with . . .'

'Yeah.' There was general agreement.

They all walked on in silence for a few moments until Billy's arm suddenly stiffened over Paul's shoulder to halt him. The others stopped and turned.

'Here,' said Billy with the wide-eyed smile of a sudden good idea, 'don't your mum and dad sell After Eights in your shop?'

Paul's pulse-rate quickened. 'I dunno,' he said. His voice had lost its strength and the words came out as little more than breath. 'I 'spect so, they're chocolates, aren't they . . .'

'Yeah, they're nice,' said Billy, and he relaxed his arm and began walking on once more.

The next silence was a long one. It lasted nearly all the way back to the school. Paul dared not say a word, wanting neither to offer nor to refuse anything, waiting for a remark Billy had kicked into the air to come down at his own, Paul's, feet, or to ricochet off somewhere. He'd deal with it if it came his way, but he wasn't going to chase and fetch it.

To his surprise it never came down. At the next street corner Billy removed his arm and with a stinging slap on the back said, 'See you,' and within three minutes the whole group had split off to get their various teas.

When he got in Paul shouted, 'It's only me,' and he made straight for the lavatory, where he could stand and think undisturbed for a few minutes. He wasn't sure whether he really needed to think this After Eights business out, whether anything was expected of him, or not; but a strange tightness in his chest somehow told him that all ways up he'd be stupid to ignore it completely.

If Arthur's grandad had been a fortune-teller and he had told Paul last night that tonight he would be thinking about nicking a box of After Eights for Billy, Paul wouldn't have believed him. Billy hadn't existed at that moment. But that had been a special oasis in time. Now the sharp memory of his previous misery, and the pattern of the days events, was leading him seriously to contemplate doing just that. It was funny how you got used to accepting the inevitable, how the mind got progressively used to an idea. Today he had come to expect more and more from Billy, and now he wanted to keep things the way they'd ended up, and who knew what he would do in order to preserve the new friendship? It was like jumping off the top board at the baths. It was a big courageous step from jumping off the pool side to jumping from twelve metres up; but if there were jumping platforms all the way up you did it bit by bit and you didn't think there was anything extra-special about your final plunge – not in the doing it, anyhow. So it was now. Having got used to helping himself from the shop, sucking on sweets to comfort him in his loneliness, and having the sort of day he'd spent the week pining for, it hardly seemed a crime to do something easy just to keep life going smoothly. It wouldn't be giving in to a threat, he told himself, because Billy hadn't threatened him. It would be just a show of friendship, a sort of good-will gesture he'd be making. Friends gave one another presents, didn't they? And he badly wanted to think of Billy as a friend. So . . .

So he suddenly stopped thinking about it, and, his mind made up, he hurried downstairs to put his head round the kitchen door.

'Wotcha.'

'Oh, it's you, Paul.'

' 'Lo, son.'

His mother and father turned from their hunched positions at the kitchen table. God, they looked shattered. Suddenly seeing them look round at him like that made even Paul, with his problems, think about someone else for a change. His mother had aged, about ten years. Her eyes, which had been known to sparkle, were dark and deep and the skin beneath them was puffed with red now the day's

93

work had worn off the make-up. Her hair, which always looked superb when it was done, and nothing when it wasn't, looked nothing. But it was the lifeless expression of fatigue on her face that pulled Paul up short. She looked like one of those young women he saw with four kids under five, old before their time, and in the face that was looking round at him Paul could suddenly see with a shock what she would look like as an old lady.

His father, a less practical person, had taken less of the toll of worry. He was tired to exhaustion point, too, but his fatigue was more physical than mental. Once out of the job he hated his frustrations seemed shallower, more to do with particular things like the broken deep-freeze than with long-term worries. His hair, beginning to grey, was still in place at the end of the day, his moustache remained well-trimmed, and he always remembered to twist his ring round to show the diamond when his hand was flat on the counter.

'Had a good day, son?'

'Yes, thanks.' Paul daren't ask them. He didn't want to hear even the slightest hint of displeasure at his not helping them again. It would make him feel extra bad about what he was going to do.

'Found some friends?'

'Yes.' But he didn't want to elaborate on that tonight.

'Hungry?' his mother asked, pushing her empty tea mug away and slowly getting up.

'Fairly.'

'What do you want?'

That was one advantage in having the shop, he knew. Feeding was easier. Everything was to hand. There was no running out of anything you fancied when the larder could extend to rows and rows of shop shelving.

'I dunno.' If Billy and the lads had been there to hear him he'd have asked for scampi and chips, just to make them laugh. The best laughs with Simon Tulip had always been in somebody's house when they could bring out all their private jokes. But they weren't here, neither Simon Tulip nor Billy. Paul was on his own once more – although the chance thought of Billy again suddenly made him realize the fantastic opportunity he was almost turning down. He took it quickly, before it disappeared.

'Shall I have a look in the shop? See if there's anything I fancy in there?' he asked the floor.

'Yes, if you like. But don't go picking something that takes a lot of cooking, will you? Nor too dear. We haven't made our fortune yet.'

'No, O.K.'

What a great idea! That was a real stroke of genius. This would save a heck of a problem. He was so relieved she hadn't wanted to come and help him choose – as she might once have done. But thankfully, for the time being, both she and his dad seemed fairly rooted in the kitchen, and he should have the shop to himself for a few minutes while he looked for what he wanted.

The empty shop had an eerie atmosphere. It had a lifeless waxworks feel to it, and with the faint shaft of light from the street lamp filtering through on to the mat by the door, the over-all effect was of a scene in a grisly murder film. It didn't take much imagination for Paul to see some sinister crook coming round the corner from the dark cubicle where the main stock of cigarettes was kept, with a stocking mask over his face ...

He didn't like it. He put his ball bag down, flicked a switch on, and a neon tube flashed into a buzzing life. That was better. The white light bathed the confectionery section, and while his heart raced – he was nowhere near the groceries he was supposed to be considering – his eyes darted along the well-stocked shelves.

They didn't take much finding. There they were, the

After Eights, six boxes built up in a pyramid on the second shelf from the top. Oh, no! That meant if he took one he'd have to disturb the pattern. But it wasn't just that. It was the price. Look at it! These were the only After Eight boxes he could see, and they were nearly a pound each! The big ones! Hell, he couldn't take one of those for a kid at school, not even for an awkward kid like Billy.

Paul hovered there, not knowing what to do. Well, that was that, wasn't it? *Wasn't it?* He stared at the long expensive boxes, glistening in their tight cellophane skins. Why did they have to be so big – special Christmas boxes, or Mother's Day, left over? Why couldn't they be the ordinary ones? He sighed. That put the tin lid on that. No way could he take one of those. Well, it'd do one thing, he told himself. It'd test out Billy's friendship, him turning up without them. It would make it quite plain whether Billy wanted him, or what he could get out of him. Paul could still feel the close weight of the boy when they'd got tangled in the playground, and the droop of the friendly arm over his shoulder. Surely that had meant something, he thought. The remark about After Eights had just been casual conversation. Must have been. Yes, casual conversation, friendly rabbiting, that's all it had been. Paul half-turned away from the confectionery shelves and for a moment he felt a bit better about the boxes being so big.

But then what about the cryptic note he'd had the day before, and the marked map? Had that been a threat, or a joke? Paul thought hard about that. He tried to bring back to mind every look he'd seen on Billy's face. But there'd been so many, and with such variety, that he couldn't tell anything by doing that. Actions were all he could go by, he decided. Well, Billy had followed up the library business by letting him play at break-time today. No, Paul decided, the map marking must have been a joke. He probably hadn't come into the shop at all.

Paul turned his back completely on the shelf of sweets. But before he could move off another thought had struck him. What about the first night in the shop when Billy had tricked them out of thirty-five pence? That couldn't have been a joke or he'd have given Paul the money the next day, wouldn't he? He'd not mentioned that since, so perhaps it couldn't all be explained away as a sort of cock-eyed friendship. Things weren't as simple as that.

What to do, then? That was the big question; and the trouble was that now he had precious little time to answer it. Someone was bound to come in at any minute.

Paul stood there, screwing up his muscles and relaxing them in an effort to make his brain work faster. Damn, damn, damn, damn, damn! Well, it would definitely pay to keep in with Billy, he thought. Yes. After all, he told himself, defiantly, his own happiness was at stake, and wasn't that something to consider? But the blessed boxes were much too big to take, that was the trouble. All right, then, what about something else? Liquorice allsorts, or something? The thoughts raced through Paul's mind as the seconds swept round the Hovis for Tea letters on the clock. No, not something else; it couldn't be, because that really would look like crawling. If it wasn't a gift of After Eights – what they'd been talking about – it had to be nothing. Oh, God, what a mess!

Suddenly a door clicked behind Paul in the house, and with a shock surge of adrenalin shooting into his system he leapt guiltily across the shop as if a gun had gone off. He grabbed a can at random and turned towards the door to meet whoever it was, trying to look casual, as if he'd been browsing along the shelves and had finally gone for this one.

Blast! He wouldn't get another chance to come in the shop on his own like this. He could sneak out a pocket of chewing-gum from under their noses, but not a big box of best chocolate mints. He stopped again and cocked his head to one side. No one was coming. He listened. It was all quiet. He had to make up his mind quickly. What to do, what to do, what to do? Paul held his breath and his eyes flicked left, to the shelf where the big boxes were. Blast the noise for interrupting him! Now he didn't even know where he'd got to in his reasoning.

So he stopped reasoning. Suddenly, he knew what he was going to do. He'd found a perfectly good reason for his next action.

Stealthily, step by step on tiptoe so as to make no noise – he was on borrowed time, he should have been out of the shop by now – he went over to the shelf and, stretching up, he gingerly removed a big box of After Eights. He took one of the bottom three in the pyramid, holding the others up with the end of his can of food while he replaced it with a box of Meltis Fruits from a nearby stack. Then he backed away.

He'd got it. He'd done it. It was too late to change his mind now. Now he'd only got to get it out.

God, the box was big when you held it in your hands. But that was all right. He wasn't nicking it. It wasn't so bad. It wasn't going out of the house for Billy. *It was for himself*. It was his pocket money. He didn't get any, so this was it. And if he should just happen to take a few mints out of the box to put in his bag for school, well then, that was his business, wasn't it?

Paul got to the shop door and slipped the long smooth box into the plastic bag with the ball in. He breathed out noisily through his pursed lips. That was done. From now on the rest, getting it up to his room, would be easy. But he never wanted that sweat again!

Leaving the bag at the foot of the stairs, Paul took his can into the kitchen and put it on the table. His mother looked very hard at the label, and even harder at him.

'Is this what you want for your meal?' she asked. 'Mushrooms in brine? Are you feeling all right?'

'Yes,' said Paul, defensively. 'I fancy those.' He'd eat anything now the danger of discovery was over.

Ten minutes later he was sitting at the table and under the puzzled stare of his mother he was pushing some of the heated food down. The taste turned his stomach, but he soldiered on and he even managed to keep going till his mother stopped him and suggested he might have been thinking it was something else.

When he went upstairs later he still felt a bit sick. It could have been the food, or it could have been the strain of taking the expensive box of chocolates. But he'd done it, and he knew he'd just have to put up with feeling sick in the circumstances.

He might have felt a bit sicker, though, had he seen the two eyes move away from the shop window a little earlier when he'd switched the neon light out – when, with his well-lit performance among the shelves finished, the chance audience had walked thoughtfully on.

Chapter Ten

THE long box of chocolate mints weighed Paul down on his way to school the next morning; not so much physically as mentally. In the cold light of a September morning it seemed completely out of place for him to be taking the thing to school. It was the sort of present you might turn up with on the last day of the year for a teacher, or perhaps if you were going to someone's party after school, but you'd be mad to be taking it for your break-time lunch, or for another kid. Not, Paul kept telling himself, that either of those reasons applied. They were for himself. The trouble was, his mother had been in and out of his bedroom that morning at all the awkward times. That was unusual these days, for a start. Whether he'd just noticed it because he'd had something secret to do, or whether she really had suddenly got a conscience about him and needed to fuss about clean pants, Paul couldn't be sure. But what he did know was that every time he slid the box out of his bag to put some of the mints in a Maltesers carton from the wardrobe top, the door of his bedroom kept bursting open and his mother kept swishing in to look for clean things. Once, he only just had time to kick the smooth box under the bed and hope for the best when the door opened. It wasn't even as if he didn't mind having the empty Maltesers carton found: his nightly feasts were still his secret. But the result of it all was that now the box was in his bag with the wrapping half off and the cardboard a bit torn, and it couldn't even be taken back home and returned to the shelf that evening.

There was one other problem. After the way Billy had

made free with his bag the day before he knew he couldn't call it his own. That meant he daren't leave the box in it. And now he wished like hell that he'd not been so stupid as to take it off the shelf in the first place. What the devil had he been thinking of? His only chance, he told himself, walking slower with every step, was to get it into his desk before school started and switch some After Eights into the Maltesers box then. He could probably keep the big box hidden beneath some books for a couple of days, until he could get rid of what was in it bit by bit. It was just vitally important that he shouldn't meet Billy before he got there. He didn't want to be forced into giving him anything this big: he wouldn't be able to lift his head up ever again. No, he certainly wouldn't give Billy the whole big box, but on the other hand a few mints in a Maltesers carton wouldn't take the skin off anybody's nose. He just mustn't meet Billy before he'd switched them.

A noisy open lorry cut through the estate sounding like an accident and startled Paul as it came up behind him. God, he was jumpy. To cover his scare he threw the plastic bag over his shoulder and broke into a run. Anyway, he told himself, the sooner he got this done now, the better.

Once in the empty classroom Paul lifted his desk-lid to shield what he was doing from unwanted eyes, and, working swiftly, with an ear cocked for the opening click of the door, he tore the wrapper right off the box and looked for the way in. Blast again! He'd never realized, not having had one before. There were two sliding drawers of mints, and in his over-anxious eagerness one of them shot out and tipped half the crisply enveloped squares into his desk. Beginning to panic, he scrambled these loose mints into the Maltesers carton and fumbled to get the inner drawer back. Hell, he'd had some aggravation over this, but thank God he was nearly done now! He looked over the top of the raised desk-lid to check the door. Good. All clear still. The minty-sweet smell of the thin chocolates rose up and surrounded his lowered head and he crammed two dark squares into the round hole of his mouth. Better than mushrooms in brine any day, he thought wryly. Great, he'd done it! Perfect. He was clear. Now the long box was well hidden beneath the school books, and the Maltesers carton on his desk top looked old enough to have just marbles or crayons or bubble-gum cards in it. That wouldn't be too flashy a gift to give to Billy.

A figure passed the classroom door and then immediately came back to check on what he'd seen. It was the headmaster, Mr Griffiths, who came into the room, sucking in behind him a swirling cloud of cigar smoke. But Paul had known he would have to be prepared for something like this, so although his heart beat a little faster, he wasn't unduly worried now that he'd got his desk-lid shut.

'Hello. Paul, isn't it?'

'Yes, sir.'

'And what brings you into the classroom so bright and early?' The headmaster came across to Paul and stood over him, tapping a football manual against his leg; he was not too close, like a policeman, but just near enough to show that he wanted some assurance that Paul wasn't rifling the desks, preserving a slight air of formality by keeping his other hand, and his cigar, behind his back.

Paul gave him his most innocent look.

'Please, sir, I've come to look up the assignment card. We didn't get much time yesterday, and I'm interested ... It's all about round here ... the estate ...'

Paul felt the situation called for a slight lift of the lid, showing willing without showing all.

'Really?' Mr Griffiths came closer. 'Have you got the card there?' he asked, looking genuinely interested.

Oh God! Paul had played his hand, and that should have been enough. The man should have gone away. He hadn't reckoned on the bloke actually being interested!

'Yes, sir, I was just looking. It's either in my desk or Arthur's . . .' Now there was nothing he could do but lift up his lid and pretend to search for the card. Already, he could feel himself going hot; he was aware of every drop of perspiration as it formed on his forehead, and yet he dared not draw the headmaster's attention to it by wiping it off. He'd done it all wrong. He should have said he'd already looked in his own desk for the card, and then they could have both looked for it together in Arthur's. That was probably where it was, anyway. Now, unless something happened to save him, he was going to have to turn his whole desk out under the gaze of the headmaster and reveal the very new looking, obviously hidden box of After Eights. And Griffiths was no fool. He'd know damn well he'd taken it from his shop without permission.

With nothing to lose, Paul suddenly took a chance. It was nothing planned; it just seemed to come to him that it would be a good idea to play on the man's interest. Quite deliberately, he shut his desk-lid, leaned on it and said, 'I think I know what the card said, though, I just wanted to check on a name.' Deception was beginning to come easily.

But Mr Griffiths still wanted to see the actual card. He was reaching out his hand to lift the lid for himself.

Paul pretended not to see the hand and casually sat on the lid. He gabbled on, desperately. 'It's about local places, streets and things. We've got to find out where their names come from, like "Cherry Tree Estate", "Toll-gate Lane", that sort of thing . . .' Would it work? He'd blown everything now.

'Oh, yes?'

Had he hooked him? Griffiths had turned and sat on

Arthur's desk. He pulled on his cigar and folded his arms. Yes, he'd done it! He must have!

'Go on ...'

'Well, please sir, that bit's easy. What's got me is the name of the flats, the reason for it. Er, Doral Court ...'

'Doran House,' the headmaster corrected.

'Yes, sir, Doran House. Only we looked it up the other night and we couldn't find it in any of the encyclopedias, and I wanted to make sure of the name. I've been thinking about it,' he lied.

'Good for you. Well, I could tell you the answer, of course, but ...'

'Oh, no, don't say,' Paul put in quickly, almost enjoying himself now. 'That'd be the same as Miss telling us ...'

'Good boy, well done. Well, you look around first. Around the streets, up behind the houses. Your parents, and Arthur's people, are newcomers, so maybe they can't tell you. But use your eyes, and with yours and Arthur's brains, you'll find out.' He suddenly got up, his fingers burned by the finishing of his cigar. 'Well done, well done.' And he went quickly out of the room, leaving the door wide open for the children coming in.

Hell, that had been a near thing! Paul slumped, round-backed, on his desk. Now he could wipe the sweat off his brow. He pulled his tee-shirt up and covered his face, wiping it two-handed, like the footballers do. God, he thought in the red glow, if I hadn't shut the desk and started gabbling on he'd have had me. Then a sudden thought struck him. Wouldn't Simon Tulip have been proud of him? And Billy! He smiled within the secrecy of his tee-shirt. Yes, Billy would have been really proud of him too!

'I can see your belly-button!'

Paul's tee-shirt was shot down quicker than a skirt caught in a gust of wind. Lorraine. Trust her! His eyes blazed into her laughing face. She always caught him with his guard down, no matter what. Somehow there seemed to be no defence against her.

She laughed again and turned to the suddenly serious Rita, who was watching them both with very sharp eyes. Lorraine sniffed.

'Here, smoke. Can you smell it, Reet? He came in to have a quiet smoke of those French cigarettes, didn't you, Paul?'

'I never. It was Mr Griffiths.'

But it was a waste of time protesting. She'd already moved on.

'Oh, how nice,' she said, opening the carton of Maltesers on the desk to reveal the After Eights. 'My favourites. These for me?'

'No!'

'For Reet?'

Rita turned away, frowning, to show that she wouldn't want them if they were.

'No!'

'Arthur? They to make up with Arthur?'

Arthur? Paul frowned. Did she think he needed to make up with Arthur? Blimey, were they all that sensitive round here that you couldn't play with who you wanted to? She was stupid. Arthur didn't come into it. He shook his head. 'No!'

But he knew she'd guess right with the next name. She was bound to be on to Billy.

'Out your shop, are they?'

There she went, off at a tangent again, always where you didn't expect her to go.

'In a way.' He wanted to ignore her, but he knew it wouldn't be wise.

'Your mum give them to you for lunch?' She had put her head on one side, and her face, too, was suddenly serious.

'Yes.'

'Oh. In a Maltesers thing?'

'Yes.' Why did his voice always come out sounding so guilty?

'Come on, then, I'll have one.' Rita had changed her mind and was reaching over to get into the act, and before Paul could get the carton back she was offering it to the newly arrived Arthur.

'After Eight, Little Arthur? Compliments of Paul . . .'

Paul turned to look at the other boy, suddenly aware that Rita offering Arthur a chocolate on his behalf could be a useful good-will gesture. But Arthur's green eyes weren't going to meet Paul's.

'No thanks,' he said curtly, and he sat down and got his reading book out. And then, Paul noticed, with a reminding roll of his stomach, that Arthur's book-mark was the assignment card he'd just done all the acting about.

'Oh, shame,' said Rita. 'No sales there. Good job it's not like that down your shop or your mum'd have to give those big boxes away . . .'

Paul turned quickly and stared into her mocking face. What the hell did she know about big and little boxes? She *couldn't* know, could she? But Rita just stared back at him, and as Paul looked next at the other girl to see what she might know, Lorraine gave an almost imperceptible shake of her head and a slow, serious, private, wink. Paul saw it with his eyes, but he felt it as a strange breathless sort of sensation inside; and he'd had to look quickly away.

'Come on, places. Reading books out, please.' Miss Simmonds was brisk and clearly determined to brook no nonsense today. Her confident tone switched Paul's mind to his immediate classroom needs. He sat down and got his own reading book out.

A new quietness settled over the room. Gradually becoming aware of it, unaccustomed to it, people looked up, looked round, and then looked down at their books again. Even the little group in Billy's corner was quiet. There was a strange new peace about the place, and it took even Miss Simmonds a few moments to analyse why. It was simple, though. And it was good news to Paul. Billy wasn't there.

With every minute that went by, as the register was called and as the late dinner money was collected, Paul's spirits rose higher. It became more and more certain that Billy wasn't just late, he wasn't coming; and that meant two important things to Paul. It meant he wouldn't have to crawl round Billy with his gift-offering after all, and he'd have a whole day with the other boys to really get in with the gang. That'd be very useful. He read a paragraph for the third time over. It was funny, he thought, how you could worry about something, and then find it didn't happen after all. But that didn't mean you didn't need to keep on your toes. Take Lorraine, for instance . . . From under lowered brows he looked across at her. What was her game, he wondered, teasing him so much, making him feel so awkward, then turning him upside down with a wink like that? She didn't seem to do it to anyone else. He raised his head a bit to get a better view of her face. When she talked to him she made him feel so awkward most of the time he couldn't look at her. But now he could see that it was quite a nice face when she was still, when she wasn't going on at him. It was smooth, peachy, and her hair curled down over her forehead like a girl on television he liked. Her teeth were very white, and . . . Lorraine suddenly looked up and caught him staring at her. Paul cleared his throat nervously, and coughed into his hands. But there was no saucy comment this time. She smiled at him, and held his look for two or three seconds before a sudden snigger from Rita spun the smile off her face.

'I know you now, Lorraine!' she said in a sing-song voice, her own face straight.

'Oh, big deal!' Lorraine retorted. She stared Rita out and Paul, covered in confusion, started to read his book through a haze of red. But he wasn't given a second to ponder on the meaning of the girls' exchange. Nothing, not even embarrassment, could last long for Paul. Situations changed swifter than expressions on a teacher's face.

'Sorry I'm late, Miss.'

It was Billy, striding in through the door like a pop singer walking out to centre-stage, not bothering to shut it behind him, and obviously not really sorry he was late at all. He led with his ace of trumps.

'I've just been talking to Mr Griffiths about the school team,' he announced with a grin which bounced all round the boys and settled on the lads at the back. 'He wants me to pick it.' He stood where he was as if he were about to call out, 'You, you, and you' right then.

'Very well, Billy Richardson. But not just now, please. We're about to go into assembly . . .'

'Yes, Miss.'

'I'd closed the registers,' she grumbled. 'Do you want dinner?'

'Yeah.'

Miss Simmonds looked up sharply from the book. 'And what else, Billy Richardson?' Her voice had a hard and meaningful edge to it. Everyone in the room knew she was waiting for the word 'please'. 'And what else?' she repeated.

'Nothing, Miss. Just dinner . . .'

Miss Simmonds scraped her chair back and shot up. 'PLEASE!' she shouted, her earlier tone of confident authority gone already. 'What about "please"?'

'Oh, yeah. Sorry Miss. Please.'

But Billy didn't turn a hair. With an annoying grin on his face he resumed walking towards his desk, taking the longer route behind Paul, and somehow accidentally catching his foot a jarring kick against a leg of Paul's chair.

Accident, or purpose? In or out of the school team Billy was going to pick? Paul couldn't be sure of the answer to either question. But he was suddenly glad that he'd come to school with the After Eights. Malteser carton be blowed! He could tell he was going to need the full big box after all.

There was nothing Paul could do till break-time. It was annoying, he thought, how you sometimes couldn't get to grips with important moments in your life, even though you knew they were coming up. He began to resent the time he had to spend doing ordinary things before he could get the box to Billy; before he could find out just where he stood. And things weren't improved when he found out he wouldn't even be in the classroom with the rest of them that morning. Out of the blue he was called with Arthur to Miss Simmonds' desk, to talk about their assignment.

'I told Mr Griffiths about it,' Paul told her, part of him still keen to please. 'And he said to look for information about Doran House on the estate. "Up behind the houses," he said.'

Arthur wrinkled his nose, the intellectual seeming to doubt even Mr Griffiths in the matter. But that was all; just the annoying wrinkle. He said nothing.

'Well,' suggested Miss Simmonds, 'why don't you two go out for half an hour and see if you can find what Mr Griffiths means?'

Oh, no! Paul still wouldn't admit to himself that he felt bad about Arthur: but he certainly didn't fancy them going out round the streets together. He'd already decided he'd insist on working with the others in the classroom rather than be on his own with Arthur in the library, and now he had to go out with him. But what was worse, he didn't like having to lose touch with Billy. This morning, he sensed, was going to be vital.

'Now, you can take a notebook if you like, but if I were you I'd just use my eyes, like a camera. If Mr Griffiths says so there must still be something to see . . .'

'Yes, Miss.' It would be no good asking not to go.

'Did he say anything else, Mr Griffiths? About the work you're doing?'

'No, Miss, not really.' Paul could see what she was on at, though. Did he say the work was a good idea? That was what she meant. She had suddenly looked almost as unsure of herself as he felt.

But she took her disappointment well. 'All right, off you go, then. I should go along Astra Avenue to start with. And back by break-time, please . . .'

'Yes, Miss.'

As if he wouldn't, Paul thought. He would never know where he stood if he missed break-time.

Arthur, a notebook and pencil prominent in his hand, walked studiously through the doorway, leaving Paul to follow him, and the two of them walked in silence to the school gate, one behind the other, like two men carrying a long ladder when only the briefest and most necessary of communications is likely to be made.

Paul thought it was going to be a waste of time. Using just their eyes, neither pushing the other on by sharing a thought or making a suggestion, they weren't likely to discover very much. So Paul kept his mind switched off Doran and he began thinking about someone else – Lorraine. That was a bit strange for a start. With Billy and the business of the After Eights buzzing in his brain so much already that morning, it seemed odd to be thinking about the girl. But he was, and not only that, he felt quite contented to be doing so.

Lorraine. He didn't even know her other name, he realized. But he could still see her suddenly serious face, a shock to him after all that teasing, and he could still remember the wink she'd given him. And what about her and Rita having a go at one another? A strange sort of warmth wrapped itself round him and made him want to smile. He actually wanted to smile. Well, that was twice this week! Once Billy and once Lorraine. Not bad for a girl, he thought. He wasn't sure what was happening, but he wouldn't mind a few more of the smiles and less of the smart remarks.

And what about Billy? He could be smiling much more from now on, if Billy's kick of his chair had been accidental, and if he could get the mints to him without a lot of fuss at break-time. And he could do it, he was sure of that. He could do it, would do it, because it was important. It could mean a place in the team, and a place in the team meant everyone knowing, from Mr Griffiths down. And everyone knowing meant security. No one could mess you about after you'd played a good game for the school team. So now it was all down to getting this stupid Doran business behind him and back to school for break-time.

He focussed his eyes again and pretended to take notice of where he was. He might as well go through the motions while he was here, he supposed. But he definitely wouldn't be a second late getting back to school.

Astra Avenue had two dead ends leading off it on the left hand side, he noticed; every twelve houses there was a gap with two pairs of houses round a corner, as if new roads had been intended to branch off but a halt had been called in the building. Across the ends of these cul-de-sacs, and in line with the bottoms of the back gardens, there ran a fence, and beyond the fence lay a field of harvested wheat. It was the southern boundary of the Cherry Tree Estate.

Still saying nothing, Paul followed Arthur into the first cul-de-sac and walked down to the fence. Was this where Miss Simmonds thought Mr Griffiths intended them to look? Hardly. There seemed to be nothing here to give any clue to an historical find; certainly nothing exciting; there were just rows and rows of hard, cut stubble and lines of machine-split stones between them, and in the far distance two never-ending columns of silent vehicles hurried between London and the south like ants between their nest and a mound of sugar. Above the field a skylark hovered, twittering its territorial claim, and all around was still.

'I don't get it,' Paul offered. But Arthur had already walked away. Paul shrugged his shoulders and followed. All right, he could *be* like that . . .

The second cul-de-sac off Astra Avenue looked very similar to the first, except that here the barbed-wire fence across the road was replaced in the middle by a long five-bar gate. This must be where the tractors come in, Paul thought. He leaned on the gate next to Arthur, putting one foot up on the lowest bar like a real countryman.

'Hey, that's barmy!' Arthur wouldn't look round at him, but Paul frowned just the same. 'They must've run out of money when they got to here . . .'

In front of them, stretching for about fifty metres, was what seemed to be a continuation of the cul-de-sac roadway, and at its far end it seemed to peter out into a two-rutted track, tractor wide. But for the entire length of the made-up surface it was as broad as two roads, extending to the breadth of the front gardens on opposite sides of the cul-de-sac.

'That's where the next lot of houses go, then,' said Paul, 'when the farmer moves out . . .'

Arthur's serious consideration of what lay before them didn't change. But he did manage to say one word.

'Rubbish!'

Paul turned hotly towards him. He could leave that out. There was no need for that.

'Well, it's where the road goes, isn't it? Doran must be the bloke who built the estate. Or the farmer. This has got to be what Griffiths was on about.'

'Rubbish!'

Paul turned back to the wide ribbon of tarmac. That *had* to be it. He said nothing more because there was nothing more to say; but exasperation with Arthur widened his eyes, as if he were swallowing something hot, and he knew that if Arthur said 'Rubbish!' once more he'd want to shut his mouth for him!

'That's too wide for a road,' Arthur said eventually, unable, it seemed, to keep his opinion to himself. 'They wouldn't put a motorway through here; and besides, it's not as new as this.' He stamped his foot dramatically on the ground, like a television reporter at the scene of an accident.

'Do you know then?' Paul couldn't resist asking the question.

'A fair idea. At least I know what it looks like . . .'

But before Arthur could finish Paul was over the gate and walking across the tarmac. He'd be blowed if he'd be out-done by this cocky kid who thought he knew it all. 'Oh, yes,' he suddenly pounced. 'So do I. Yes,' he said again, as he walked farther away, 'definitely.'

'Well, what?' Arthur called.

Paul stopped, and then he wished he hadn't. He hadn't expected to be asked. He hadn't thought Arthur would bother. This was the second time today his bluff had been called.

'Roman road,' he said flatly. 'Probably discovered by this bloke Doran . . .'

Arthur's immediate and sardonic laugh brought Paul as close to really hitting him as he'd ever been. It was very close. He could take a lot, but he couldn't bear being laughed at like that.

'Is that what you think?' Arthur eventually forced out when his shoulders had stopped falsely heaving. 'A *tarmac* Roman road?'

But before he could burst out into another bout of acted uncontrollable laughter, Paul cut through the mesh of his pretence.

'Nuts!' he exploded. 'As if I bloody care anyway!'

And he suddenly broke into a fast run back to school.

Chapter Eleven

IT was a stroke of genuis, Paul reckoned, getting the mints to Billy the way he did. From the start he'd ruled out the possibility of the ideal opportunity arising – like being on his own in the classroom with Billy and being able to hand the box over with a casual remark like, 'Do you fancy these?' He'd known that wherever he did it there'd be other kids about, that it had to be public, and so it wouldn't have to be clever. But he hadn't thought he'd be quite so convincing in the lie he told. He didn't even know where or when the lie had come to him. It just came; and he just said it.

When the buzzer went for break-time, a few minutes after he got back, Paul, looking at no one, but quite openly, took the long box out of his desk, tucked it under his arm, and walked over to the cupboard for his football bag. Then he went out into the playground and walked purposefully round behind the kitchen to where the game was played; but before anyone could start playing, he slid out one of the drawers and started offering the After Eights around.

'Here y'are, have a chocolate,' he said. 'Have a couple. My mum's birthday. After Eights all round!'

'Oh, cheers, son.'

'Ta, mate.'

' 'Ere, that's big ain't it?'

All the footballers, Trevor Dalton, Mark with the hair, stocky Ron, and the rest, they all helped themselves to two, or three, or a wedge of four, and flicking aside the small brown envelopes into the swirl of dusty litter, sucked the flat chocolates into their mouths. Then Paul walked over to Billy, who was standing there waiting, bouncing his own football in the goalmouth.

'Here y'are,' said Paul, finding himself unable to call the boy by his name. 'After Eights, my mum's treat, on her birthday . . .'

For a second or so Billy looked at him. He gave away nothing by his eyes, just a long expressionless stare while Paul watched his face. He might help himself, or he might bounce his ball up and under the box to send the chocolates flying. Either way was possible with someone as unpredictable as Billy.

Paul was just beginning to feel foolish, standing there all that time, offering them to the other boy, when Billy spoke.

'Oh, After Eights,' he drawled at last. 'What I like. Ta.' And he took one mint, in its tight envelope, and put the whole thing in his mouth, paper too.

Paul smiled his most tolerant, quizzical, smile. What did you do to that? But he had only to wait three seconds to find out. You had to duck, for Billy had a way of eating After Eights all of his own, a little trick of extracting the mint from its wrapping with his tongue and then shooting out the paper like a missile. It just missed Paul, who laughed, tactfully.

'Oh, very good.'

Swallowing quickly, Billy took another one and did it again, and this time Paul made sure the paper missile hit him on the cheek. And that, Paul judged, made the moment right for him to make his big move. He gave the whole box to Billy.

'You can have these,' he said as off-handedly as he could manage; 'I don't like 'em much, and my mum won't want me to take them home; it's her birthday . . .'

'Yeah, you said.' Billy took the box and put it down by

one of the painted goal-posts. 'How old is she? Ninety-nine?'

'No!' said Paul. 'A hundred!' and he dribbled the ball away fast, so as not to hear whether Billy laughed or not, so as not to see the expression on his face. Paul felt rotten and disloyal inside; but he quickly consoled himself with the thought that she couldn't hear him – only Billy had heard the remark – and only the two of them knew he'd just given up another bit of his self-respect. Well, *he* had to make his way at school, not his mother. And he badly needed this friendship, he badly needed to be part of an easy relationship where a crowd of you team together, made mistakes, and shouted, 'Never mind, mate,' like the men had at the football. So making a harmless joke about his mother couldn't hurt if it helped a bit, could it? He dismissed the last trace of an uncomfortable feeling with a good hard kick of the ball.

He had to wait until the end of break before he could get round to putting the big question to Billy. But at last the moment came, and as the other boy stooped to pick up the long box of After Eights from beside the goal Paul asked as casually as he could, 'You playing tonight, Billy, over the park?'

Billy stood up and shot him with a quick, appraising, glance. 'No, it's Thursday, ain't it? We're loading up special for Rochester market.'

'Oh, yes.' Paul nodded, as if that explained everything to him. He didn't mind not playing if the others weren't.

'But there's a game tomorrow. Straight after school. School team trial.' He put an After Eight in his mouth and blew the paper out ahead of him. 'Teams goin' up in the morning,' he mumbled.

Paul's heart began to feel bigger inside his rib-cage and he breathed in loudly. It was hard to believe, but it was all beginning to happen, at last, more or less as he'd planned . . .

The two boys sauntered across the playground, Billy eating the mints and shooting the papers carelessly on to the tarmac, Paul silent, and thinking over, between feelings of elation at everything coming good, Billy's remark about Rochester market. Was his dad a market trader, and Billy one of those lucky kids who shouted the odds on Saturdays? He seemed the type, when you came to think about it, forceful, with a loud voice. They got as far as the steps before Billy spoke again. He tucked the box under his arm and said in a quiet voice, without the slightest hint of force or menace, 'Yeah, I like these After Eights. Almost as good as one of those big round things of Turkish Delight, I reckon.' Then, deliberately not looking at Paul any more, he turned to the others following behind. 'Don't forget. Teams go up tomorrow. Bring your boots, all of you. I'm ònly 'avin the one trial . . .'

It was blackmail. There was no other word for it. So it was down to that now, all out in the open. All the excuses Paul had tried to make as reasons for Billy's behaviour were rubbish. It was bringing Billy in a box of Turkish Delight, or kiss good-bye to a trial for the school team. It was as simple as that. And that meant – in this place – kissing good-bye to having any friends like he'd had before. It was deliver the goods or make the best of cocky Arthur.

Wrapped in moody insensitivity Paul stumped into the classroom, bumping unfeeling into the walls and other children until he got back to his desk. He'd gone out here with so much hope, and now here he was, back again where he'd started, with nothing settled except the undeniable fact that Billy wanted to be paid his dues. He swallowed. That fact came hard to a kid who'd thought nothing of carrying Simon Tulip shoulder-high round the playground, helping him call for his men to fall in and follow.

Paul didn't remember much about the next hour. It was some sort of a shambles, with Billy pushing his luck to the brink of Miss Simmonds' tolerance, while the rest of them tried to write a story. Paul attempted to repeat a success he'd had at the other school, a fantasy about a man who controlled everyone with a giant robot, but he couldn't concentrate, he left all the best bits out, and it ended up as only a pale reflection of the original which had really pleased his other teacher. He was still rubbing out something wrong when the buzzer went and Lorraine efficiently scooped the four books away from their table and put them on a corner of Miss Simmonds' desk. Too fed up to protest, Paul got to his feet. He was clearing off out to a quiet corner somewhere. He hadn't taken a step, however, before Lorraine had returned to the table and thrust a bundle of newspapers into his arms.

'Here, what . . .?' he began.

'Miss said you can help me put out the paper for art,' she informed him in her not-to-be-denied voice. 'Rita goes home to dinner Thursdays, so it's you.'

'Oh.'

Well, at least it was something to do instead of worrying about whether he should play football with Billy after dinner. Paul started slowly spreading the sheets of newsprint across the nearer desk tops, and gradually the classroom emptied until even Miss Simmonds had gone. Children's voices became distant, and as Paul worked his way over to the window where Billy sat, the sun warmed in through the glass and the faintest feeling of well-being permeated the air. Perhaps it was the mild sense of power at finding himself standing over where Billy sat, in a position to break the boy's pencil or put his Maths book in someone else's desk; perhaps it was the sun on his shoulders, giving through the glass what it could seldom give to the gusty grey estate outside; or perhaps it was the presence of Lorraine, moving about the room in time to a favourite song. Perhaps it was the combination of all three, but just for a moment, Paul felt a bit better.

'Oh, I like him, don't you?'

Paul looked up from the page of Stock Exchange prices he'd laid out on Billy's desk – the most boring page he could find for him – and looked over to the paper which Lorraine was holding up. He saw a stripped-to-the-waist footballer to admire.

'Oh, Arsenal!' he said. 'Rubbish!'

'I think he's got a lovely smile,' Lorraine went on, turning the page round to look at it again herself. 'Look.'

Paul didn't really want to, but Lorraine got her own way by walking over to him with the open page and spreading it on top of Billy's. She leaned over it close to Paul.

The man was certainly good-looking.

'He missed a penalty Saturday.' But Paul knew they were talking about two different things. She wasn't on about football. They stood there next to one another looking at the smiling face, and Paul began to feel a slight reluctance to move away and finish his job.

'You never said you had a whole box full,' Lorraine suddenly said, still staring at the newspaper. 'After Eights. You just had a few in that Malteser carton.' She turned and looked at him, her eyes somehow soft and challenging both at once.

There was no way he was ever going to relax in this place. 'Oh, I just put a few in there ...' Paul started talking quickly, sounding confident, but without knowing he would finish what he'd begun. 'It was ... it's ... my mum's birthday. She gave me a box to share out at school, so I put some in the other carton, right, so as not to look flash. But then I thought it didn't matter so I got the big box out ...' None of it made much sense but he hoped he was saying enough to satisfy her. It was all lies, anyway, but lies he was somehow beginning to believe in himself, as if the reason for giving Billy the whole box had already begun to go from his mind. Like a kaleidoscope the bits and pieces of his life at school kept on getting changed by the shakes people gave them.

'You didn't nick them for Billy, then?'

Eh? God! 'No!'

Lorraine's voice had been quiet, confidential; it hadn't been the brash tone she used in front of other people; but there could be no possible way of softening what she had actually said. She was on to him; she knew; and he knew she knew.

Paul had to swallow. He fought against the involuntary action as being an admission of guilt – or at least of embarrassment – but he had to do it, and the quieter he tried to make the swallow the louder it came out. His face, he knew, was either a deathly pale or violent red; he could feel the changes tingling beneath the surface of his skin. And he knew he'd been well understood by this girl.

'No, I done it for a joke ...'

He stared down unseeing at the footballer on the desk top. There was no way he could look her in the eye.

'You aren't afraid of him are you?'

Again, the soft question, but less challenging; her voice already hinted at her own disbelief that Paul could be afraid of Billy.

'No, of course not!' Now he *could* look at her. He had to, because he was on sure ground here. It was only this school team business, getting in with the lads, that gave him any reason for playing up to Billy; it wasn't the fear of getting a punch on the nose, or anything like that. At least, he didn't think so.

Lorraine was looking at him straight in the eye, and all he could see were her own wide, serious eyes, with just a vague impression of the rest of her pale face, her dark curly hair and her white teeth.

'You don't want to be scared of him, Paul. Not you. Not like all them other cissies are. They've all been scared of him since they were infants. But you've come down from London . . .'

She did know, then. She knew what he was about. She knew what he'd expected. And obviously she saw the lad from London as someone who was himself expected to upset the local apple cart. Paul said nothing. Some moments always left him without the words to cope with them.

Neither of them seemed to want to move. They were both still leaning over Billy's desk, and Paul, looking down again, noticed the underside of her arms, turned forward in the attitude of the lean. They were shining and smooth. He'd never noticed anyone's arms before.

'Well, don't do nothing else stupid for a joke, will you? I don't want you to get into no trouble . . .' Her voice was very low, very confidential, very special.

'No, all right . . .' Paul had to clear his throat to finish saying those three words. It was stupid how she could make him feel so awkward. But suddenly the last thing he wanted to do was to move away. He felt a new and almost pleasant feeling of discomfort, a pain he didn't want to go. There was something about this moment which was like swinging higher than ever before, when your stomach goes over and the swing makes new and unfamiliar noises, something about standing here alone in the classroom with Lorraine which seemed to rob him of his ability to breathe properly.

But nothing lasts for ever, and as the distant shouts of the dinner ladies for the second sitting heralded the end of their moment of quiet, Lorraine suddenly leant even closer to him. Paul tensed himself but he didn't move.

'Excuse me!' she said in her normal perky voice, and she whipped up the footballer from under Paul's hands and ripped it in two. 'No. I don't think I like him after all,' she said. She crumpled up the paper and threw it under the desk. 'His eyes look a bit shifty to me . . .' And she walked out of the room to dinner.

Paul would have sat on his own at dinner – amongst some younger kids at any rate – if he'd had the choice, if only to give himself a chance to think before committing himself too quickly to any particular course of action. But Mrs Lock bustled him in on the table where Billy was sitting with the others, and he found himself in no position just then to make a stand against the other boy by shunning him. In no time he was lassoed into their conversation with the noose of humour – he never could resist a smart remark and a good giggle – and in spite of himself he nearly fell off his chair laughing at Billy's hilarious description of Miss Simmonds getting to bed at night, taking out her teeth and her glass eye and unscrewing her wooden leg; and it somehow only seemed natural to follow that up by playing football with him again, both after dinner and during the afternoon break. Besides, he decided, there was always the chance something might be said to let him off the hook.

He thought Lorraine had seen him being ushered against his will on to Billy's table, and she certainly steered clear of the football games afterwards, so he didn't feel bad about her. But since Billy said no more about Turkish Delight, one way or the other, nothing changed there; and almost before he knew it that afternoon he'd painted a rubbishy picture to go with his rubbishy story, home-time had arrived, and he was avoiding Arthur at the gate and walking back to the shop, still trying to sort out the tangle of old arguments and new emotions which filled his head.

By the time he got home Paul had just about settled on offering to help behind the counter again. But he was surprised to find that the shop was shut. It was Thursday, early closing day, and the whole parade had that closed Bank Holiday look which always depressed him with its deadness.

Something about the stillness told him not to knock at the side entrance, so he went round to the gate and through the concrete back yard to the kitchen door. It was open, and almost stealthily now, he let himself in to the tap-dribbling quietness within.

This was something new. Every afternoon since they'd been there his parents had been in and out of the shop, serving or restocking, banging doors, scuffing boxes, slamming the till. Now it was all too uncannily quiet to seem real. Surely they wouldn't have gone out and left the kitchen door unlocked? And they couldn't be tied up on the floor, could they?

Suddenly concerned about what he might find, Paul walked across the hall and opened the door into the shop. No, they weren't in there; the only sign of life was the buzz of electricity in the freezer cabinets. He went out again and cautiously opened the door into the living-room. Like all quietly opened doors it clicked and creaked loudly, but not even the suddenness of Paul's intrusion could wake the still figure lying on the settee. Norman Daines, covered with a car rug, was breathing the shallow sighs of unconscious exhaustion. Paul, silently, blew out his own relief. That meant Mum was up on the bed: the Sunday afternoon pattern from back in London. Something was getting near to normal, anyhow.

Caught now with the door open, and afraid to move his

feet on the thin floor covering, Paul wasn't sure what to do. He could tip-toe up to his own room and get out a game of something; he could sit in the kitchen and watch the tap drip; or he could go out to play. Oh, hell! He had always hated those Sunday afternoons when he had to be silent, when his parents' sleep was the family's first priority. It had never seemed fair to him, although the usual car ride afterwards, the summer-evening drink in a pub garden, had always restored the balance. But it took only a few seconds standing there thinking for him to suddenly realize that today he could actually use their siesta to his own advantage. He could tuck into a few favourites from the shop. And he might even have a look at the Turkish Delight, just see what the situation was, the sizes, the prices, in case he should decide to seek some final treaty with Billy; some very definite and very final armistice.

What an opportunity to have staring him in the face! Now it was vital for him to close the living-room door silently. It'd be a crying shame to wake his dad up now. Shifting his weight slowly, like the spy-comics said, testing the new area of floor before trusting it with his weight, he turned and, centimetre slow, he pulled the door to behind him. The final shut made an unbelievably loud bang in the silence of the house, but no voice called, and, after a few seconds pause while his pulse rate quickened, Paul prepared to enter the empty shop. So far, so good, he thought.

Unseen to him, though, the figure on the settee in the living-room began to stir, and a sleep-dry mouth triggered the thought of sweet tea to a tired but waking brain.

Paul had been on the top deck of an empty bus and had the feeling of wanting to sit in all the seats at once; he had run into a park of fresh snow and wanted to make marks all over it; and now, in the empty shop, with little fear of discovery, he wanted a mouthful of everything sweet at once. He didn't know where to start. The wideness of the choice before him pulled in so many different directions at once that it tethered him there in the doorway, and he couldn't move for a good five seconds. But at last, with precious time lost, he went for quick convenience.

The loose boxes were the easiest to manage, the wine-gums and the liquorice allsorts, but those were hardish sweets and they didn't give the instant satisfaction of soft-centred chocolates or fruit jellies, so Paul compromised, and moving swiftly up and down, he filled his pockets with wine gums and his mouth with unwrapped chocolate truffles, letting the sweet dark taste seep down between his teeth. And only then, with the first rush over and his chewing beginning to slow, did he stand still and start to think.

He could see the Turkish Delight on the shelf, there for the taking. There were several of the round wooden drums piled up, with the top one turned on end, none of it looking like a special display of any sort. Paul could picture the contents, thick white paper enveloping the soft heavy cubes of pink and white, a little fork for lifting them out, and a liberal powdering of fine sugar settled over the top.

Suddenly, it seemed to be a tempting take. Being easy to lift was important, but more than that was the importance of what it could do for him. It could get him the one chance he needed, a place in the trial – the once-and-for-all action. There'd be no more decisions like this to make after this last one. Just this once, Paul thought, and he'd be in where he wanted to be for good. It certainly was a tempting take.

While he cleared his mouth of the last trace of chocolate truffle Paul leaned on the counter and looked across at the shelf. It would be very easy. The pile of drums was well within his reach; one of them wouldn't be missed;

and he could slip it into the looseness of his shirt front and have it up in the safety of his room within a couple of minutes. Yes, it would be very, very, easy. He looked down at his tee-shirt. It was loose enough already; he wouldn't even have to ease it out.

But as he looked down Paul suddenly noticed the odd angle of his arms. It was strange how, when you were leaning forward, the inside of your elbow joint twisted round to the front, he thought. Perhaps he was double-jointed. But no, that couldn't be, because if he was, then so was Lorraine, for her arms had looked like this when she was leaning on Billy's desk.

Lorraine. Paul hadn't wanted to think about Lorraine. He had deliberately tried not to consider anyone else but himself in deciding what to do about Billy. But he'd done it now. He looked down at his arms again. They were like Lorraine's; although all arms were much the same, he supposed. But as he looked at his own he half-closed his eyes and pretended he was seeing hers again, in that pleasant interlude in the classroom; his were perhaps not quite so rounded, and they were certainly more tanned than her white skin; but there was the same smoothness there ... It really was strange how he had never noticed anyone's arms before.

Lorraine would know about the Turkish Delight. She would know about him giving it to Billy as she had known about the After Eights. And then what would she think of him? She might think he was afraid of Billy, not the bold boy from London any more: and then in her eyes he'd probably be the same as the other kids who'd all been under Billy's thumb since the infants.

Well, did it matter? Why the hell should he have to be thinking of this now? Was it any concern of his what some girl thought? Was he going to start going all cissy, playing skipping with the girls while the boys played football? Not likely! But then Paul thought again of that quiet moment in the classroom. It was probably the closest he'd ever been to talking privately like that with anyone before. He remembered the way he had felt, his stomach turning over with a new pleasure and his heart beating fast; the unusual softness of her voice; the serious eyes; and he remembered one thing she had said in particular. 'I don't want you to get into any trouble . . .' *She* didn't want *him* to be in trouble. She'd been trying to say that what happened to him was important to her, as if she really cared about him.

Oh, hell! Now he felt all mixed up. He'd just got everything sorted out in his mind: what he'd wanted to do, and how he was going to do it. And all these stupid new thoughts and feelings kept draining his intention away from him. Why the hell should somebody like Lorraine affect him like this?

He didn't know what to do any more. He looked again at the drums of Turkish Delight. It'd be so easy! And yet . . . Slowly, almost reluctantly, he turned away.

'Paul? Is that you, Paul?' It was his father, yawning and scratching in the doorway. 'I thought I heard a noise.'

'Yes, so did I,' Paul said quickly. 'But I've had a look. It's all right in here.' He looked along the shelves. 'Everything's O.K. as far as I can see . . .'

Paul felt bad about his decision later. Once both his parents were up and about, busy again in the closed shop, and the Turkish Delight was beyond his grasp, he kicked himself for not having taken it. Surely he could have got it to Billy in some secret way, which still left him in the clear with Lorraine? Why couldn't he have the best of both worlds? Now, having played Billy along so far, he'd just thrown away his final chance of making sure of his Cherry

Tree place. He'd gone soft for a minute, and look what happened!

It had been a weird mixture of a day, filled with tension and sugared with pleasure. There had been the scare with Mr Griffiths first thing, the unpleasant search for clues to Doran with Arthur, the giving of the mints to Billy, and then the blackmail bombshell. And there had been those quiet, pleasant, moments with Lorraine. It all left Paul feeling more mixed-up and strangely uncertain than before; and something else still nagged at him, something still unexplained that he wasn't happy about: something had happened, or been said, that had been passed over, left unresolved and he didn't know quite what it was. The more he thought about it, the further away it went. It was like trying to remember someone's name. But still it wouldn't come. Something apart from Billy's blackmail was worrying him, and he didn't know what it was.

It didn't come to him until his mother asked him to go outside and empty the doorway litter-bin. And then he knew. Oh hell he knew! As he looked back into the lighted shop the answer came to him at once. Of course! He kicked the bin in a red haze of frustation. He was a stupid idiot! Stupid, stupid, stupid! Somehow Lorraine had known he'd nicked the After Eights, hadn't she? And she must have known either because she'd seen him, or because she'd been told by someone who'd seen him. And that was it, the nagging worry. He'd been seen. He'd had the light on in the shop, and his movements had been seen just like his father's could be now, just as clearly as if he'd acted them on the telly. And so that meant Lorraine could think he was just scared of being seen again. And although she couldn't expect him to do more than he'd done, there was still no way she could know about his big decision in the shop.

Back in his room Paul laid on his bed and stared at the

darkening yellow ceiling. It would need something more positive on his part to put things as right with Lorraine as he would really like them to be. Playing football well in front of her, that would have been a way; but playing a brilliant, courageous game of football was definitely out for him now. And what else was there? What was flash and brave and just for her?

He closed his eyes and gave his mind over to wild imagining. Lorraine in distress and saved by Paul. Perhaps those white arms waving out of the sea as she was swept out of her depth, and him cutting through the treacherous waves to pull her safely back on to the beach; and then going to see her in hospital, and her saying thank-you.

Or Billy threatening her, refusing to let her go home from Victory Park until she'd given him some money to buy sweets; and Paul walking up and telling him to let her go; pushing him aside, and with a straight left knocking the wind out of the big boy . . .

And with his mind taken off on such flights of pleasant fancy, Paul fell soundly asleep in his clothes where he lay.

Chapter Twelve

THE next morning, Paul Daines began learning really
fast. He learned that you made your own luck, and that
what you did came down to what you'd already done to
help make it happen. Billy, for instance. He'd been right
about him. He hadn't been fooling. It really was, 'No
Turkish Delight, no trial for the football team'. A few
meaningful looks across the classroom, with Billy even
shaking the empty After Eights box to his ear, had been
just preliminaries to the make or break moment in the
playground when Billy clearly expected to be given the
expensive sweets. He had led the way unhurriedly round
to the football game, slowly enough to be caught up by
anyone who wanted to catch him up, and he had lingered
a while before the kick-off, but with precious playing time
passing, the game had to start without Paul's payment,
and without Paul.

Paul, for his part, hadn't been sure what to do with his
time. Lorraine had gone off with Rita, without looking in
his direction, without so much as a glance to show
whether she knew what Paul had done, and he was left
feeling lonely again, and rather foolish in the undramatic
daylight. Real life was very different from those fantasies
projected on his bedroom ceiling. Thank God thoughts
were secret! He began to wonder where Arthur went at
break-times these days: they had done no more work on
their project, and now Paul felt wistful even about their
shared morning in the library earlier in the week. At least
there had been something genuine in that: a bit of com-
radeship. But he wouldn't go looking, and in the end he

was left to walk alone around the playground perimeter, keeping out of everyone's way, pretending to have a deep interest in the vehicles passing by.

This was miserable, he thought as he looked out through the railings. For just a mouldy box of Turkish Delight, he could be round there on the other side of the kitchen knocking a ball about, getting called 'Paul' and 'mate' and being counted in as one of the school football squad. Instead of which he'd played up to that Lorraine and now he'd been left high and dry by the lot of them. It wasn't fair. It wasn't stinking fair.

The climax, the final word on the Turkish Delight, came after break in the classroom as everyone trooped in from the playground. Billy walked round behind Paul's tense back and stopped there.

''Ere, Daines, ain't it your dad's birthday today? Sweets all round, like your mum did?'

Lorraine wasn't back yet, and neither was Arthur. Paul turned quickly in his chair. 'No, it's tomorrow,' he was very tempted to say, better late than never. But that somehow seemed worse than having brought them, like pleading with a blackmailer for time to pay. If he was out, he suddenly decided, he might as well be right out. 'No, mate,' he said, 'you got it wrong didn't you?' He turned back to the table which was still empty. Pity. That he'd have liked Lorraine to hear . . .

Billy, his face the picture of 'don't blame me', moved on without a further word to Paul. But as Miss Simmonds hurried into the classroom he called out loudly, 'Miss, tell the boys the teams are goin' up for the trial tonight. On the board down the corridor.' He smiled his power around the room before sitting slowly at his desk. But Paul didn't need to look at any notices. He could already guess what the details would be as far as he was concerned. And he would have just sat there, morose and self-pitying and only pretending at his work, if Billy hadn't then pushed his luck too far.

All the week Billy had been whipping up a frothy atmosphere of unsettlement in the classroom, the sort of disturbance Paul's old teacher would have allowed just once in a new class before putting the tin lid on it. Although she was nominally in charge of the class, Miss Simmonds found order hard to maintain – and Billy and company had been quick to realize how reluctant she was to show her lack of control to Mr Griffiths by keeping her threats and sending anyone to him. So from time to time there were shouted exchanges, and scuffles even, which Miss Simmonds pretended not to see or to hear. Today was Friday, though, the strain was telling, and what might have been excused on Tuesday was definitely not going to be overlooked today.

Miss Simmonds was seeing more people about their assignment cards, and since it was Friday she was leaving everyone else to finish off uncompleted work, to tie up the frayed end of the week's activities. For some it was Maths corrections, for others spellings, but for the majority it had got back to silent reading.

One by one the pellet notes came flying through the air. It seemed impossible that Miss Simmonds shouldn't see them, but with one or two children sometimes obstructing her view, and with Billy's sense of timing, the impossible was achieved for quite a while. And in spite of himself, Paul couldn't help watching the display with a sickened sense of loss. He would have been in on all this, he thought; he would have been in the thick of it at the other school, with a teacher like this. But all he could do here was sit and watch from the sidelines.

Billy was sitting with his head down over a torn-out notebook, looking as if he was getting on with his work – and only the scanning eyes beneath his lowered head gave any clue between the shots to what he was really up to. But suddenly, when Miss Simmonds' head was down, Billy's would come up, with a pellet in his teeth and a rubber-band taut, and with a swift turn of the head in the right direction he would let fly with the faintest of thin pings. Then within half a second he was back over his book, looking the picture of innocence, until he could safely check his accuracy a few moments later.

Paul watched the boys who received their notes obeying their instructions. One at a time, waiting till their routes were clear, they shuffled like cowboys in the scrub across to Billy's desk, and after hurried consultations they returned to their places, smiling gratefully. It was all about the football trial, obviously, probably telling them they were in it; and from who they were Paul knew damned well that on ability alone he should have been one of them. He began to loathe Billy with a new, sick, deep, loathing as the boy flicked his power all around the room, a new depth of loathing that even all the aggravation that week had failed to reach. How dare that ignorant swine leave him out? And what sort of a rotten school was it where the whole business of the football team was left to an animal like that? They were all idiots around here, everyone, all the estate in their horrible houses, Griffiths and his stupid cigars included. And even Lorraine, sitting there solemnly next to Rita as if he didn't exist today, even she couldn't be excluded from his feeling of bitterness.

But just then Paul was forced to stop his embittered thinking as Billy, over-confident, tried a shot too clever. It was the trick shot a lot of them had been waiting for. Ricky Marshall, a small nippy boy on the fringe of things, sat at the desk right in front of Miss Simmonds' table. And it was highly likely he'd be in the team out on the wing. He had to have his note the same as the rest. Billy's pride was at stake, and the dodgy shot definitely had to be made.

Billy would have to lean out into the aisle to make it, but it would be a straight shot then, down the length of the classroom to Ricky, who had to be trusted to intercept it before it carried its flight on to land like a wasp on Miss Simmonds' desk.

A slight hush fell over the room as the attempt was made. A few nervous giggles had to be impatiently shut up by Trevor Dalton as Ricky, smiling over his shoulder between repeated checks on Miss Simmonds, shifted his seat to give himself maximum mobility. Then Billy levered himself out into the aisle and with a wide monkey-like grin, the pellet in his teeth, he took aim. Everyone was looking either at Billy or Miss Simmonds. Nobody breathed. Here it went.

Soundlessly, like a dart from a blowpipe, it shot down the aisle. Ricky Marshall had positioned himself nicely, holding up a hymn book to bat it down. No sweat. It was going to be easy.

But Arthur had chosen just that moment to show his own frustration at these childish classroom antics. At the end of an exasperated rooting in his desk to clear out a pile of mint wrappers someone had stuffed there, he accidentally dropped his desk-lid ten centimetres. Crash! Down went the lid, and up shot Miss Simmonds' head, just as Ricky Marshall lost his concentration for a split second, and ping! the pellet went stinging painfully into the teacher's cheek.

'Who did that?' Miss Simmonds was on her feet instantly, her hand to her outraged face. 'Billy Richardson, come out here!'

Billy stood up slowly, frowning at her injustice. It wasn't him. Hadn't he been quietly getting on with his work?

'Hurry up! Come here!' Miss Simmonds' voice shrieked her absolute disgust at these hooligans who seemed bent on proving her uselessness at her new job. She didn't get this sort of thing down at St Joseph's. In sheer desperation, to give her hands something to do instead of taking the swing she wanted to at the oaf of a boy before her, she opened the thick pellet.

Ricky M., it read. *Trial over Victory tonight. Report to me now.*

'How dare you use my lesson time to organize your stupid football?' Her eyes blazed behind her thin-rimmed glasses. 'Stand on your chairs all the boys who are in this!' She held the note up in a shaking hand. 'Come on!' She was doing her utmost not to notice Billy lounging loutishly by her desk. Shocked and stinging, at that moment she would gladly have lost her job over the unmanageable boy, but some last degree of professional cool came to her and she kept her hands away from the insolent head.

Gradually, one by one, red glances flashing across at one another, the boys with notes stood up on their chairs, some looking sheepishly at their feet, others staring hard at Billy, who'd got them into this. No one, Paul noticed, seemed to put the blame at Arthur's door by so much as a flicker or a glance. But Arthur was conspicuous in another way. With Fat John and Paul Daines he was one of the few not included in the trial.

'I was only getting all my men organized,' Billy said sullenly, 'like I'm s'posed to . . .'

'And what do you think you are? A trade union leader?' Miss Simmonds shouted at him. 'I'm in charge of this class. And if you think flicking paper pellets round the room is an acceptable way of getting organized, then you've got another think coming!'

Paul swallowed. That phrase, 'all my men', Simon Tulip's and now Billy Richardson's, struck home painfully. For a box of Turkish Delight he could have been one of Billy's men. And quite safely, too, because with so many of them involved Miss Simmonds wouldn't do much about this. Instead of which he wasn't anybody's man; not Billy's, not Arthur's, not old Simon Tulip's; and not really even his own.

Billy began to grin and the lads on the chairs grew more relaxed as it became clear that Miss Simmonds was only blustering and she really didn't know what to do next. But like one man they all suddenly shot up straight as Mr Griffiths came hurrying in to check on the football arrangements with the team captain, tearing the situation out of everybody's hands.

'What's going on here?' he demanded, covering the space at the front of the room in three long angry strides. 'Have all these boys been misbehaving, Miss Simmonds?'

'Well,' Miss Simmonds began. She really wanted to isolate Billy as the ringleader, for the others weren't to blame as he was. But she was denied the chance as Mr Griffiths sped round the room looking at the work in front of each of the standing boys. 'Is this all you've done?' he was demanding. 'Not enough, laddie! Not nearly enough! This is disgusting for a morning's work!' He moved on swiftly to the next, and the next. 'They've obviously not got enough to do, Miss Simmonds! How dare you boys be so lazy in my top class?' He returned to the front of the room. 'Sit down! And bring me three pages of best handwriting, each and every one of you, by hometime this afternoon. And woe betide anyone who fails!' And he walked angrily out of the room with a critical slam of the door.

Secretly near to tears, Miss Simmonds stood Billy in a corner with his back to the class and tried to pick up the threads of her work. But the buzzer had gone before she could sort herself out enough to get down to anything again.

'Paul and Arthur, I want a word with you,' she said quietly as the rest of the room walked out, the most subdued it had been all week. Then she went out of the room herself for a few moments, and Paul was left to sit silently next to Arthur until she returned.

It was an awkward couple of minutes, and not just because Paul was wondering what she could want to see them about. It was the sudden embarrassment of sitting there on his own next to the boy he'd been ignoring for three days. It was being left alone with the kid whose friendship he'd thrown over to keep in with Billy. And for the first time since he'd decided not to go back to the flats with Arthur, Paul was secretly prepared to admit that he might have been a bit more friendly.

Now he began running through a few things he could say, perhaps an apology for not turning up to see his grandad's pictures. But he couldn't really concentrate; he was still smarting over Billy, and again the words wouldn't come. So he sat there with his hands crossed flat on the desk and, finally abandoning the attempt, he began to wonder again what Miss Simmonds could want. Was she going to pin the blame on one of them for banging the desk-lid? No, that wasn't on. She couldn't have known. She hadn't seen. Did she want them to tell her something about the other boys? Well, he'd never been a tell-tale. But what else could set them apart like this, except the fact that they weren't in Billy's gang?

Well, there was only one way to find out; so Paul stuck his legs out straight, crossed them at the ankles, folded his arms, and silently waited.

When Miss Simmonds came back she was wearing a pair of tinted glasses and her sharp nose seemed a bit red, but otherwise she was quite brisk and matter-of-fact as she walked over and sat down on Lorraine's chair to speak to them.

'Your project, that assignment card,' she said. 'You two seem to have made a good start with it. Probably better than most . . .'

The boys said nothing. There was little you could say to something like that.

'Well, now, how's it coming along? Have you got any further?'

Paul looked at Arthur, and Arthur looked at Miss Simmonds.

'I've managed to do a bit more on it,' Arthur said, 'on my own at home.' He gave Paul the smallest of sharp, meaningful glances. 'I think I know what was up on the field now, but I haven't been able to link it with Doran yet.'

'Good.' Miss Simmonds nodded her approval and then she looked at Paul.

'I think I know,' he said. 'I've been doing a lot of thinking about it . . .' He hoped to God she wouldn't ask him what he'd come up with: a tarmac Roman Road certainly seemed a bit unlikely; and since he hadn't improved on that, he'd look really small if his bluff was called.

'Well, look,' said Miss Simmonds, 'I think I can tell you two this. I happen to know that Mr Griffiths is very keen to see how you get on with it. He was very pleased to find out that we were doing a project about the estate. But as you know, quite rightly, he doesn't like time wasting. Now, at my other school the children were quite used to working on their own in the way you started to do, and they went on to using tape recorders and cameras and all sorts of different things for recording what they found.' She looked around the room at the vacant desks, clearly comparing their occupants with her old class in her mind.

'But here some people think you need to be told every little thing you have to do, every minute of the day . . .' She paused again, and it didn't take a great brain to realize that she'd got her own settling-in problems. 'But I think you two could prove them wrong.' Then she shut her mouth firmly and got up. 'That's all.' Perhaps she thought she'd said too much. 'I certainly think you're two boys who could show how my idea could work, if we could just spark an interest and the others would give it half a chance. Now over the week-end I want you to think how you could really make this come to life. Show us all what could be done. All right?' She smiled, bravely, like a cabinet minister under attack on television.

'Yes, Miss.'

Picking up a loose pellet from the floor, and dropping it distastefully into the paper basket, she went. And so did Arthur. Paul, left sitting there completely on his own, swore softly. This was bloody marvellous, he thought. Talk about the Lone Ranger! And, worse than that, he was one of the good boys now, in with Arthur on the side of the angels. He hoped to hell Simon Tulip never found out about this.

Chapter Thirteen

PAUL wished he'd got a bike. They hadn't been too
common in his own built-up part of north London; they
were forbidden in the parks and vulnerable on the busy
roads, and most people seemed to live without them without missing them. But now Paul began to realize why so
many of the kids around the Cherry Tree estate had their
own transport. On a fine day, like that sunny, windless
Friday afternoon after school, it was the only escape from
the dusty boredom of those restricted semi-circles of
planted trees. If you weren't going into Victory Park, or
catching a bus to Eastfleet, all you could do was patrol that
familiar pattern like an animal in a cage. So the answer
was a bike, which could get you away into the lanes in minutes and give you the freedom of the countryside – surely
the only possible consolation for not living in the town.

Avoiding the keen shouts of the boys arriving in Victory
Park, Paul found his feet taking him out towards Astra
Avenue and the cornfield. But it was no random choice.
As he had found, every action stems from something that
has happened before, every action a reaction, and so he
found his path chosen for him by what he wanted to avoid
and by what he wanted to find. If he was on the side of the
angels at school – and it certainly wasn't his choice, he'd
want anyone to know that – then he was going to need more
than a bit of bluff to offer Miss Simmonds on Monday. In
the gambling language his dad used to use when he'd had
some friends round, Miss Simmonds had 'called' him, and
he was going to have to show a higher card than he held at
present. He simply didn't know what he'd pretended to

know, and now it was down to him to find out. After all, there was another world apart from the playground, and succeeding in that could be important, too. In his shoes now he'd got to believe it!

Doran was a man, he was pretty certain about that, and Mr Griffiths had made it clear that the clue to his identity lay out here on the edge of the estate, 'behind the houses'. That meant the cornfield. And the implication was that it just needed a keen eye and a bit of brain to put two and two together and come up with an answer. But deep inside Paul knew there was an easier way of finding out than making an aerial survey or going on an archaeological dig. With Arthur and his grandad not here to criticize him, all he had to do was ask someone. Everyone knew but the newcomers, it seemed, and surely he could catch someone in their front garden and get an answer. And then, after that, according to what he found out, he could play it by ear. At least he could come up with something to tell Miss Simmonds on Monday. He'd be pretty damn stupid if he couldn't. And, God knew, there was nothing else for him to do around here.

But as Paul walked along Astra Avenue towards the gaps in the houses, the only people he saw in the front gardens were little kids, and only two of them, and before he'd had the chance to find anything out he had daydreamed about a bike until he found himself at the farmer's gate.

Paul put his head down on his arms, leaned on the gate, and stared out along the tarmac strip. Of course, he could see now that it wasn't Roman: not because of the tarmac; anyone could have put tarmac on top later, so Arthur needn't have wet his knickers laughing at that suggestion; but because it was too wide and flat. The Romans would have put more camber on it, and they wouldn't have made it so wide. But it was dead straight, and that surely made his idea at least a possible one. Perhaps if he got a map and lined it up he could see where the road came from and went to. That would be something he could do for a start.

Moodily, he sucked a red patch on his left arm, and he stayed like that for a while, wiping it and then sucking new areas. Hell, he was fed up with everything about this place. He didn't seem to get anywhere with anything. He was bored, browned-off, frustrated. But he had to admit to himself that there was a certain peacefulness about leaning on a farm gate and staring out over a country field. He shifted his weight and put his head lower down on his arms. The reddening sun still warmed his back, and he smelt the warm human smell of his own skin.

'Oh, hello.'

Lorraine's voice suddenly came into his mind. It was the warmth on his back and the smoothness of his arm that made him think about her, and in spite of his bitter thoughts that day he found himself slowly smiling at his mental picture of her.

'Don't turn round, then!'

She laughed, and then it hit him like a prod in the spine. The voice had been real, not in his mind at all! He shot round to face her, his mouth open and his embarrassed mind willing her not to have seen his secret smile.

'You've made your arm all red.'

Paul looked down, rubbed the arm briskly and held it behind his back. 'Where did you come from?' he asked.

Lorraine said it slowly, as if to a baby. 'I live here, that house over there.' Without looking round she pointed to the house next door but one to the gate. Then she laughed, a light, amused sound that Paul liked until she spoke. 'But you know that. That's why you came up here, hanging around. I wondered when you would . . .'

Paul could only stare at her. This was unbelievable.

143

There'd been no clue to this at school, had there? In her eyes he might as well have not existed today. How you could be misunderstood! But at the same time he somehow didn't mind too much if she did think he'd been secretly nosing in the register, not with her head set quizzically on one side like that.

'That's right, isn't it?'

Paul shrugged and tried to look both non-committal and knowing at the same time. He kept his mouth shut. Sometimes it paid to be a man of few words.

'You should've knocked. You're not afraid of my mum, are you?'

'No . . .'

'Anyway, what shall we do?'

If Paul had been just imagining this his eyes would have widened in surprise; as it was, he looked hurriedly about him, not sure whether he wanted to find an escape route or not. Hell, this was an unexpected twist. People were definitely different down here: and it wasn't just the bikes. Things like this hadn't happened back in London, had they? Perhaps they had, and he'd missed out so far. Anyway, what could they do? He didn't know. His mind scrambled over ideas like a marooned swimmer over rocks, and he stared blankly ahead until time forced an answer out of him. He groped at the roadway in front of him like a life-line. Anything would do.

'I wanted to walk out there, see where it ended. Are people allowed . . .?'

''Course. Come on.' Her jeaned legs were astride the gate in no time, and before he knew it she had her hand held out to help him over.

Paul didn't need it, but he allowed himself to be steadied as he got over, and only the thought of some kid at an upstairs window made him drop it quickly before they started walking slowly along the tarmac road.

'The farmer doesn't mind. He can't. It's a public foot-path over to the other side and out to the main road . . .'

'Oh.'

'Didn't you see the sign?'

'No.' So much for using his eyes and keeping his wits about him.

They walked on in silence for a while. Now that he was out here with Lorraine, out of the sight of Billy and Rita and the other kids, Paul felt again the same sense of pleasure he had experienced in the classroom. Strange, but it was almost as good in its own way as lacing up his boots to play football – and it had the added relish of being a pleasure he would definitely want to keep private from the rest.

'You didn't take him any more sweets, then?'

Super-responsive at that moment to any gesture, sign or word, Paul turned swiftly towards her as they walked.

'No!'

'Oh, I'm glad, Paul.'

Her voice was soft and dark, like the chocolate truffles.

'Yes, well . . .'

'He's all right, really. He just has to think he's the boss all the time. Once he know's he's got you down he's all right. I think it's because he's so big . . .'

Again Paul turned swiftly and looked hard at her face. Was there a hint of admiration there? Did she secretly like Billy? It was quite possible. A sudden stomach pain of jealousy hit him with a feeling more intense than the glow of pleasure it replaced. Was she just using him to get at Billy, to make Billy jealous? Could she just be tagging him along until she decided to drop him? Paul couldn't tell anything from her face, and even when she smiled at him he wasn't sure. It somehow made him think of something else he'd been involved in; and it didn't console him to realize, as they walked on in silence, that it was his own treatment of Arthur that he was thinking of.

Paul's feeling of jealousy didn't fade until they came up to the crumbling end of the built-up roadway.

'The path goes across to that hedge,' Lorraine said. 'But the farmer's ploughed it over. It's rough, but we're allowed.' She gave him her most matter-of-fact look. 'I've got my sandals on. If you want to go over there you'll have to give me a hand.'

Paul, silently taking her hand, decided that they would continue to the other side. It was that, he thought, or turn round and go home and feel more unsettled in his mind than ever. But within seconds he was feeling very grateful to the uneven ground. He really couldn't remember anything as nice as holding her hand, swaying with her this way and that, the two of them laughing their way across the stubble. Like a headache after Disprin, his jealousy had gone without him being aware of it going; his spirits suddenly rose and sang with sheer pleasure, and like the skylark, exuberantly present somewhere above their heads, he wanted just to hover there and make the moment last indefinitely.

All too soon, though, with a final hand-in-hand leap, they had cleared the shallow ditch which skirted the field and landed sprawling on the bank beneath the hedge. It was funny, Paul thought, how an ordinary everyday thing like going across a field could be so much more enjoyable with someone like Lorraine. There was an added dimension of pleasure which being alone together gave. When everything you ever did seemed to lead to loud comments, it was good to be on your own with someone you could talk to a bit privately. With Arthur there, or Rita – or even Simon Tulip – it wouldn't be at all the same, they'd all be trying like mad to show off in front of the rest.

'Mind out, Paul.'

Just using somebody's name like that could be nice, and nobody seemed to say 'Paul' as nicely as Lorraine.

'Paul, mind out . . .'

'Eh? What? Oh, yes.'

He twisted quickly and saw the drop behind him, a metre-deep trench with rusted corrugated sides.

'Thanks.'

He peered closer at it. At first he couldn't make out what it was. With his back to the ploughed field the trench ran along to his right for about ten metres before it ended. The sides were uneven and caved in, and judging by the hummocky floor it had been much deeper than a metre at one time. At the far end the rusted wire ribs and the crumbly side of a reinforced concrete pillar stood leaning in the earth like half-excavated remains. Paul stood up and walked over to look at it. Close up, he could see that the exposed pillar was one of two, both sides of a sunken doorway into a collapsed burrow in the bank.

'It's like one of those old air-raid shelters we used to have in our garden,' Paul told Lorraine.

'That's right. It's a bunker.'

Paul looked over at her. Lorraine was leaning with her head thrown back to catch the fading warmth of the late summer sun. With her eyes closed Paul felt free to stare for a moment at her, and again he felt that new, close, private moment of sharing. But when the silence lasted she suddenly turned and squinted at him.

'A bunker? Out here? Why?' Paul turned his head swiftly back away, out to the open field and the distant stretch of wide road. And then, staring extra hard, he suddenly saw it. From this side of the field he could see back along its length better, he could see between the gap in the houses where its straight line happened to continue; and suddenly he knew.

'It's a runway!' he said. 'A bit of an airfield, an old aerodrome or something!'

'That's right,' the girl said, casually. She looked with closed eyes once more at the lidded red of the sun. 'Didn't you know?'

'Not really, no.' He turned back to the bunker. 'But what's this?' he queried. 'Was it war-time?'

'Yes,' she said. 'I think so.'

'Oh.'

Paul walked back slowly and sat down next to her, his eyes held fascinated by the abbreviated runway, his mind imagining for a moment the outraged roar of a fighter as it sped across the field towards them. So that was it. Up behind the houses. A war-time airfield. Battle of Britain, like the films. Then Doran must have had something to do with the R.A.F.! Perhaps he was the leader, or a fighter ace, maybe a hero like that bloke without legs.

'The lady next door said there was a lot killed up here, in the raids . . .'

'Yeah, I bet . . .'

For a minute they both sat staring out across the field savouring the sadness of feeling sorry, their hands deep in the long green grass, while the pleasant buzz of insects, the late afternoon songs of the birds, and the distant drone of home-bound traffic along the London road all at once seemed to make a nonsense of any thoughts of violence. Only the remembrance red of a scattering of late poppies along the field's edge and the sharpness of split concrete persuaded Paul that there could be any connection between this peaceful place and the unthinkable horror of death.

'I was watching you when you did it.'

Now what? Couldn't he ever feel settled, at peace with himself. He seemed to have to pay in some way for every small moment of pleasure he had. But he knew what she was on about. Hadn't he really guessed the other night when he'd gone outside the shop and looked back in?

'I was looking through your shop window. Not for the purpose. I was going past to Guides when the light came on; and it was you . . .'

Her voice was confidential now, low and almost conspiratorial. But it didn't make him feel any better, not when the subject was his private plot to keep in with Billy.

'I saw you take down that big box of After Eights, and I thought it was for your mum. But you looked round at the door. And you looked so *guilty*!' She giggled. 'You was lucky I was on my own. If Rita'd been with me I expect we'd have banged on the window and shouted!' Then suddenly, surprisingly, in a move which made Paul catch his breath and sent a tingle across the surface of his skin, she found his hand deep in the cool grass and squeezed it. 'Here, don't look so sad.'

Paul, careless of his deep blush, turned and looked at her sun-squinting eyes.

'I thought about it on the way home, and I knew you must have a good reason. I had to pull your leg a bit till I knew, but when you gave the lot to Billy that was it. I thought he must be bullying you because of his dad . . .'

'His dad?' What was this all about? Paul had never even met his dad. How could his dad have anything to do with it?

'You know, he's got the mobile grocery. Comes round the houses every week.' Then she laughed. 'But I suppose you won't have seen it. I don't suppose he bothers to call on you . . .'

Paul smiled, but it lacked feeling. Of course, that explained a hell of a lot. No wonder Billy thought Paul was an enemy on sight, if their parents ran rival businesses.

And even if that weren't really the reason – if it was really more basic, boy against boy, as Paul suspected – then it could seem an acceptable reason to the others . . .

All at once Lorraine's hand was gone and his own was cold in the grass. Anyway, Billy's dad or not, how could Paul really explain why he'd done what he had? It all seemed stupid, looking back, as if he'd been scared of standing on his own feet. And to himself it began to look selfish, too, all that worrying about how Paul Daines would fit in on the Cherry Tree estate, without a thought for anyone else. He let out a long pent-up breath. How did he explain that awkward embarrassing reason for doing what he had? Perhaps it was easier to let her think he'd just been scared of Billy. At least that could be explained, and understood.

'Come on, Paul,' she said. 'Forget it. My dad'll go potty if I'm late for my tea.'

She sat there and held both her hands out for Paul to get up and pull her to her feet. He accepted the invitation, and he kept hold of one hand to help her back over the rough ground. But there was less swaying and laughing on the way home, and all too soon they'd walked along the short stretch of runway and with a final, ' 'Bye, Paul; see you!' she had disappeared indoors, and taken the sun with her; while Paul, feeling chilly across the shoulders, was left to walk home, one moment trying to cherish the fleeting memory of a held hand, the next remembering the words of a private conversation which had somehow gone wrong, a chance to explain himself which had been missed. Well, he thought in consolation, he'd never been brilliant with words, had he? So he'd just have to show her, somehow. He'd have to show her beyond any doubt that he really wanted her friendship. He'd already done one thing: he'd turned down a place in the trial; but she didn't know about that, and that didn't matter any more.

Now he'd just have to find some other way of showing her how important her friendship was . . .

An hour later it was a real scream that dragged Paul's mind from another day-dream and took him downstairs towards the shop. It was his mother, and it had sounded much worse than the normal scream of her seeing a spider. It was longer, it stopped and started again, and it made his dad shout. A sense of sheer urgency hurried Paul through the doors at top speed and prepared him for whatever ghastly sight he might see. Was she hurt? Had she had some terrible accident? Was someone there, hooded and terrifying in a corner of the shop? Paul couldn't stop to think. He was dead scared, but he went into the shop and round the counter as if he were a commando.

He wished to hell he hadn't when he saw what it was all about, when he got his first glimpse of what she had thrown from her frightened hands to the floor. She was leaning back against the counter, sobbing, heaving, and trying to stop herself by banging her clenched hands on the formica, while his dad stood back, prodding it with the stick end of a fishing net, and swore between his shouts to his wife to control herself.

In the centre of the floor lay Paul's nightmare: a long, expensive, After Eights box, just the outer case, and from where he was he could see sticking out from it the tail of a dead pigeon, crawling with a new life. Something someone had scooped up from a gutter.

'Why the hell . . .?' asked Norman Daines, still not wanting to stoop closer and touch it. He turned quickly to his son. 'In the letter-basket . . . just lying there . . . Mum thought they were bad and someone had pushed them back through the door . . . But for God's sake, a dead bird! Who the hell'd do . . . It's not your idea of a joke, is it?' He suddenly turned on Paul frowning. But Paul could see him dismissing the idea as soon as he'd thought it. He knew it wasn't possible Paul would do something as thoughtless as that.

Paul just shook his head. He had gone a deep crimson, he knew, and he had to swallow just to stop his eyes from watering. There was no way he could find a voice just at that moment. Fortunately, in all the noise his missing voice went unnoticed.

Of course he'd done it. Not directly, of course. But he'd caused it, he knew. In responding to Lorraine instead of to Billy he'd left the other boy to make the next move. And now it had all come back and hurt his mum most of all. If he hadn't started it all by taking the stupid box in the first place none of this need have happened. If only he'd been man enough from the start.

Paul went over to his mum and put his arm round her waist; a gesture of comfort, and a secret apology.

But it wasn't just the dead pigeon, Paul thought as he felt his mother's sobs. This unhappiness went a lot deeper than that. She'd hidden it as best she could but hadn't he known she wasn't really keen on this from the start? He knew expressions of hers which were really full of enthusiasm and pleasure, laughs which she gave and gay responses to things, like party invitations and going out for a meal, which were miles different from the put-on pleased expressions she used at other times – the acted pleasure, like when his dad announced a week-end fishing trip for them all. And the shop business had been like that. She'd done it for his dad because he'd been up to there at the drawing office. But she'd given up a lot to do it. Her old friends and habits for a start. And it had been a bit the same for Paul. These last few days, except for those moments with Lorraine, had been bloody awful.

So his pleasure at what his father said just then almost

overcame his guilt at the After Eights box and the pigeon.

'Well, that's about it, isn't it? Three weeks' hard labour, next to no sleep, all the worry, all that smiling and bowing and scraping, and then one of our delightful customers pushes that little lot through the door. That's it! I mean, I've had it up to here! Pack the bags, Maur; we'll put this place up for sale in the morning.' He kicked the box into an open cardboard carton and stuffed some packing fibre on the top. 'What a charming place to live!'

It was the sort of thing Paul had wanted to hear ever since they'd got here. It still wasn't too late to go back to the old house, he knew, and his dad could always get some other sort of job, couldn't he? And then perhaps things would get back to normal between them all. They'd get back to being a family again. Lorraine had given him the glimmerings of a reason for staying; but that could only ever be second best to going back. Couldn't it?

'You are ... without a doubt ... the stupidest man I know!' Maureen Daines forced Paul to stand aside as she stood up off the counter and thrust her angry face towards her husband. 'For the first time in your life you have a chance to be the boss, and because it's hard going at first, and some stupid yobo or other decides to show us the sort of mind he's got, you're ready to chuck it all in and call it a day!' She took a step towards him, and Paul took a step back. She was shocked, and angry, but after those first few words her exasperation with him lent strength to her voice. 'I'm your wife and I followed you here, and I've worked bloody hard alongside you to make a go of this. And I'll tell you now, I didn't want to come. But I did come, and if you think you've uprooted me and turned my life upside down, and left Paul to fend for himself and stopped me feeling like a human being so that you can chuck the towel in at the first bit of bother, then you've got another think coming! All right, you've worked hard, and so have I, remember; but we're not doing so bad financially. Perhaps a good little shop assistant might make all the difference. But we're not starting to talk about giving up. Not yet. Right?'

Norman Daines wiped his moustache with the back of his hand, and his choked smile almost crinkled. 'Yeah. O.K.,' he said. 'I just thought . . .' There was a very long pause. 'I'll put this on a bonfire,' he finished, eventually.

'You do that.' Maureen Daines was smiling too; a bit bravely, but she meant it. 'Anyway,' she said, 'I don't remember selling one of those big boxes of After Eights, do you?'

'No, I can't say I do . . .'

The Daineses looked at one another. But not at Paul. They couldn't. He had already crept quietly out of the shop.

Chapter Fourteen

SATURDAY was grey, a drizzly, indoor day at first, with Paul mooning about the house while his parents were busy in the shop. After the big family decision the night before he'd have liked to help serve in the shop again, just to show whose side he was on, but he didn't offer in case Billy came in to see what effect the dead bird had had, and Paul knew that he was in no position to denounce him. All the After Eights business would come out if he did that. And he wasn't going to put himself under Billy's thumb any more. So he took a Mars bar from the hall, and sat down in front of the television. He saw some of the programmes and he day-dreamed through the others; sometimes his face was frowning and at others it had a pleased smile; but it wasn't until some Girl Guides came on that he admitted to himself what he really wanted to do. He badly wanted to see Lorraine. He'd never have dared let anyone like Simon Tulip know; he'd never have lived it down. But he still had to prove himself with her, and it was pointless letting a whole day go by, just remembering and worrying. When he saw the drizzle had stopped he couldn't get out fast enough. He cleaned his teeth, he brushed his hair, and after a secret splash of his dad's Brut, he put on a denim top that made his shoulders look wide, and in no time at all he was up in Astra Avenue, leaning nonchalantly on the farmer's gate, staring intently out along the disused strip.

Although it wasn't the most important thing in his life just then the runway had begun to hold a strange fascination for him. The more he'd thought about it, in between everything else, the uncannier it had seemed. Just thinking of what had gone on there, the scrambles into the air, the dodgy landings, the crashes, the gun-fire, the lives and the deaths, gave him a funny feeling, especially when he thought that here it still was, or part of it, for kids to play on as if it were nothing special, or for a farmer to use as hard standing for his tractors. It didn't seem possible.

But that wasn't the real reason for Paul being there, and his backward glances over his shoulder at a near-by house would have given him away had anyone been watching. He waited patiently, moved about, whistled, let himself be seen, but nothing happened. He conjured her voice, her image, but she didn't appear this time. Her house looked dead, shut up and gone away, with no car outside and the curtains drawn – and after the breathless high of anticipation at the thought of seeing Lorraine again, his spirits sank low at the emptiness.

In a series of casual glances he took in every detail for future day-dreams, the colour of the drawn curtains she'd be so familiar with, the small front garden where she sometimes played, the cat under the privet who saw her every day. And he suddenly realized that he felt jealous of them all. Yes, jealous, that same sort of feeling he'd had about her and Billy: a bit like feeling hungry and a bit like feeling scared.

Where could she have gone? Would she be long? Was it worthwhile waiting for a bit? Dare he knock for her and make sure? He didn't know what to do. It was hard to believe that this very place had been so full of pleasure for him the afternoon before, so drab and dead today. Fed up, he picked up a stone and threw it as far as he could down the runway. No, he wouldn't knock. No one was in. He blew his breath out in a long, drawn-out sigh. It was back home, then, and the telly again.

'Did you want something, son?'

Paul spun round, his heart suddenly going as if he'd

just run up six flights of stairs. Her mother, was it? Oh, cripes! But it was the woman next door, standing up straight behind her gate like women next door did when they were sorting you out. He'd just had the polite question before he got told to clear off, he knew that.

It was then that something he'd learned that week came to his assistance, nothing short of a brilliant flash of inspiration. He hadn't done too well by being Paul Daines so far, so how about being someone else for a minute? How would someone clever handle this old girl? What would a brainy bloke like Arthur say?

Before he knew it he was doing a very good take-off of Arthur seeking after the truth, walking slowly and seriously towards the frowning woman.

'Well, yes, actually I did want something,' he said as he approached her. He pressed his nose at the bridge like Arthur did when he was showing he was thinking. 'I'm doing some research at school into this runway thing, the airfield, and I'm sort of measuring it. Estimating,' he finished, with an Arthur nose-wrinkle.

'Oh, yes? Wasn't you up here yesterday, with next door ...?'

So she was one of those net-curtain biddy's, Paul thought. Wouldn't miss seeing a dog pee in the street. Well, if she knew about Lorraine he'd use her too.

'Yes, as a matter of fact, er, Lorraine and me are working on the same, er, work ...' He knew he'd gone red at actually saying her name for the first time. But there was no time to bother over that.

'Oh, I see; oh, well, that's all right then, son. Only I'm keeping an eye for them while they're down the caravan. And you're doing lessons about this?' She kept her hands on the gate, gesturing towards the field with a slight toss of her curly grey hair. 'What, history is it, now? Bli', it doesn't seem possible ...'

'No. Yes. We're trying to find out about the names.

Local studies ...' Paul began to move off. She was definitely friendlier, and she'd told him what he wanted to know. Lorraine was away at a caravan, then, probably for the week-end. So now all he had to do was get away smartish while he was winning.

'I've got some old stuff on all this, you know,' the woman suddenly said. 'I've shown it to Lorraine before. Funny she never asked.'

'Oh?' Paul hesitated. You never knew when you were going to be lucky, did you? 'Not about Doran, and that?' he asked, taking a chance.

'Oh, yes, all that. Is that what you want? I kept it all, what they printed in the local. Well, we used to live in one of the old farm cottages then, alongside the airfield, before all this lot was built. Billeted officers, my people did, till that day. You know, the day that Doran business happened ...'

'He's what we're finding out about. Doran.' Paul was himself again: excited, and one up on Arthur. He didn't need him now so he stopped wrinkling his nose. 'I couldn't have a look at it, could I? Sometime?' One evening after school, with Lorraine, would be ideal. A really good excuse for coming up here and arranging to knock for her.

But the woman was half-way up her front path. 'Certainly you can. Come on, son. I know just where to put my hands on it. I always have been for a good education ... because some of us weren't always so lucky, you know ...'

So Paul followed Lorraine's neighbour into her house, and under the watery gaze of an old man smoking in the corner, at last he had the story of Doran spread out before him, in yellow clippings on the dining-room table.

Sunday was sunny again, and with a new girl assistant already in the shop, getting practical advice from his mother before she put the dinner on – a real roast dinner – Paul whistled off out of the house in a happier frame of mind than he had the Sunday before, and he made his way to Victory Park. The bird business seemed to have been forgotten; and when he thought about it, Paul felt pleased that at least it had forced his parents to take on the extra help they needed. And with the full story of Doran to tell Arthur if he saw him, Paul was off in search of a football match again. It was pointless going up to Lorraine's, he knew, because she wouldn't be there and he'd only have to explain his movements to the lady again. And besides that, he half wanted to see Billy now. It wouldn't take a lot of provocation to force him into settling a couple of scores. But mainly, if he were honest with himself, it was the football he was going for. Something to talk to his dad about at dinner time, to whet his appetite.

There was a game: and, as chance and a small league would have it, the local team's opponents were the London Docks side of the week before. This week was special, though. Even as he walked through the gates Paul could tell that it was different today: a notice chalked on a piece of cardboard on the gate announced it as the first round of the League Cup; but more than that; there was a noisy and festive atmosphere inside the park; the sun was shining and the dockers' wives had turned out in force. They stood down the near side of the pitch in a bright array of coloured sun-tops and fading tans, while their daughters trotted on and off the pitch and their sons kicked about behind the far goal.

Paul knew they must be visitors by the line of cars he'd passed in Orchard Road. He looked about for local support, more than ready to deal with any situation Billy might create: but there were only a few children and one or two grandfathers to represent the Cherry Tree estate; and no wives; the dinner still had to be cooked when the team was playing at home.

Paul was drawn to the noisy side of the field as the London whites dropped their cigarette ends into the grass and trotted out to the freshly marked pitch.

'Come on you Whites!'

'Up the dockers!'

'Show 'em what you're made of, boys!'

The voices were shrill, excited, and proud; and the children looked at their mothers with new eyes. But the team kept its solemn face. This was a game they had to win, for everybody.

These Londoners knew how to treat the big events, Paul thought, Londoners always did, and he couldn't help wishing his dad was out there on the line shouting too.

Well aware that he was in for a hectic morning, the referee got the game going quickly, and responding to the urgency of the whistle it started with a fast, energetic, rush: each team going hard after the early goal which would give so much psychological advantage. The ball bounced inaccurately off the bumpy pitch; heads and legs reddened fast; and the sweat of effort in the sun soon soaked the players' shirts.

From the relative cool of the touch-line Paul stood and watched the opening exchanges with a strange mixture of feelings. First, and deepest, was that strong sense of partisanship with the Londoners, the men in white who tackled strongly and shouted loud encouragement at one another. 'Well run, Eddie!' 'Never mind, Ronnie, son!' 'Good ball, Alf!' This was what they'd taught him before, the need to let one another know they were appreciated, the strength of their feeling of belonging together. 'Come on,' he heard someone shout in a lull, 'let's hear you *talking*!'

Then, with another sort of strangely envious feeling, Paul was very much aware of the wives. They shouted and laughed a lot, but every now and then, perhaps not always appreciating the complexities of the game, they fell a bit quiet. And then Paul could see their serious eyes, following the individual men they'd really come to watch. One of them, a young woman with long blonde hair, stood a little apart from the rest and hardly said a word; but her eyes followed every move of the number ten, and Paul felt strangely envious as he pictured himself out there, playing brilliantly, with Lorraine on the line talking to no one, just watching him.

The half-time whistle went without a goal being scored, and the Whites walked off to a burst of whipped-up cheering from the touch-line. But now, with the game stopped, Paul suddenly felt lost. He wondered if the manager would remember him from the Sunday before, the boy who'd taken the orange out to the referee; but the men were all grouped over by the wives and children, and Paul didn't want to risk looking like a hanger-on, so he stuck his hands in his back pockets and wandered off round the pitch. If he went slowly enough he could make his circuit last till the start of the second half.

But he only got as far as the strip of grass between the far goal and the green changing hut.

'Would you be kind enough to give me a bit of a hand?'

The voice was embarrassingly familiar. Paul badly wanted to walk on as if he hadn't heard; but the voice was too close behind him, and there was nothing he could do but look round.

It was, as he'd known it was, Arthur's grandad. The Major stopped and stood there getting his breath, making no pretence about his need for a blow, letting his hands hang straight by his sides while he took two or three deep noisy breaths. Then he began to unfold a pressed handkerchief, shook it open vigorously, and loudly blew his nose.

It gave Paul a few awkward seconds in which to brace

himself for the Major's first words when he realized whom he'd stopped. The old boy was entitled to be cross, Paul knew that – what with a pork chop wasted and his photographs got down for no reason – but even that admission didn't make the thought of a ticking-off any easier to bear.

However, the Major either didn't remember him, or he had decided to ignore Paul's rudeness, for there was no remonstration.

'Well now,' he went on when he'd got his breath back, 'what I want to do is to get up on that pavilion thing and take a few shots of this football.' From out of a black leather case slung across his shoulder he produced a heavy looking camera with a long, large lens. 'I'm bored stiff so I've dug this out to keep me out of mischief, and what I'm after are some shots from above to see if this lens is still as good as I remember it . . .' He was patting the camera with his free hand as he spoke, as if it were a new piece of secret military equipment. 'I can get some good shots of the field of play from up there, with a clear line for closing-in on one or two of the chaps when they're running with the ball. Just for fun, you know, just for fun . . .' Paul stood looking at him, nodding and waiting. 'Look, I've pushed a bench pretty close to that side window there, and if you'll hold the camera I can shin up and you can pass it to me . . .'

Paul only needed to take one look at the bench and the window to know that it would be impossible: he'd never get up there. It wouldn't be an easy climb even for a kid, so there was no way this old boy would do it. But he played him along for a moment: there was no sense in making him feel useless. 'Yes, O.K., if you like,' he said. The old boy would kill himself if he fell back off there. 'But I reckon it's best if I go up and you give me a bunk. If you'll let me take a couple of pictures with it. I'm not strong enough to bunk you up, and I don't reckon you'll get up there on your own. None of us can . . .'

The Major smiled, and gave in quickly. 'That's what we call good use of available manpower in the army! Well, all right, Paul,' he said, 'but I don't want to hold you up if you're here with some friends . . .'

Paul. He'd remembered his name! So he did know who he was. But once again Paul could find nothing to say that would help the situation in any way, so he just bent his head down closer to the camera in the Major's hand in a sort of silent invitation to be shown how it worked.

The Major responded. 'Well now, the first thing people always have to remember is that operating the camera is the easy part. It's what you do with it that makes all the difference.' He held the camera up at Paul's eye level. 'The film is already loaded so all that's required is a squeeze of this button here. Then you move the film on with this lever here. The aperture, the amount of light you let in, is set automatically, so then the only thing you have to worry about is the focus. Well now,' he turned the camera round so that Paul could see the viewfinder, 'when the figures look sharp in here they're sharp on the photograph, do you see? It's what we call focussing through the lens . . .'

Paul looked across at the sprawling Whites and their standing wives. They made a perfect picture in the small viewfinder, crisp and colourful, like a Sunday scene on the television.

'Now you can alter the focus with this.' The Major guided Paul's fingers on to the milled edge of the lens, twisting it a fraction to the left. 'This changes the focal length.'

Immediately, the little group in the viewfinder lost the sharp edge of definition, not blurring completely, but becoming slightly fuzzy, like a child's photograph.

163

'But here's the beauty of this little fellow. It's a tele-photo lens. That means you can get in close without being close yourself; it's used a lot in action photography. Now, commencing with a general sharp focussed view, if you move the lever forward you can close-in on any figure you want, keeping it in focus all the way, and take your picture when you're ready.'

Together, they turned the lens this way and that, and then the Major took his hand away to leave Paul on his own. Paul zoomed the lens in on one of the women, the quiet one with long blonde hair. The picture was clear and sharp, and he kept on closing it in until her head filled nearly half the viewfinder.

'Well, how about that, Paul? Easy, eh?'

'Yes,' said Paul. 'I reckon I can work it.'

'Good man. A few shots from up there will give me an idea whether the thing still works. But listen ...' The Major put a hand on Paul's shoulder. 'Instructions.' He turned Paul round to where the local team, the Cherries, were stamping their feet and preparing to restart the game. 'Red number seven, he's the chap to watch. Keep a fairly wide shot of any likely looking Red attacks, they'll be coming towards you, but when someone slips the ball to seven, that's the time to close up. Get in tight on him and stay with it. That's where we'll get the shots worth having. The winning goal. You mark my words.'

Paul nodded, but he didn't quite understand.

'I don't know a lot about this game of football, but I've noticed him. A good man to have on your side, I'd say. You watch him. He's a jolly good team player when it suits him – but when he thinks he stands half a chance he completely disregards all that damned shouting and hollering, he puts his head down over the ball, and runs at his opponent and dares them to beat him. Not afraid to go it alone. And if he ends up on his backside on the ground he doesn't mind.' He clapped Paul on the shoulder. 'Yes, you watch him. Every outfit needs one of him, one chap with the courage of his own convictions, someone who's prepared to go down in the attempt.' The Major stood with his head back and waved an arm airily across the pitch. 'Whites haven't got one, you see; that's why Reds should win. Now come on, up you get . . .'

With a helping hand Paul got up on to the slightly sloping roof of the changing hut, and when he had found himself in a safe position he reached down for the camera.

'Keep yourself relaxed and try not to wave the thing about. Good luck, now.'

Paul murmured thanks without looking down. It felt heavy: the camera in his hand, and the responsibility he'd been given.

The whistle went and Paul gave the game all his attention, but it became meaningless to him as a game; thinking so much through his eyes he didn't hear the shouting of the players and their wives, and only the sharp focussing before each shot had any meaning for him.

But before the game was over Red number seven was to present him with something special to think about.

He was a clever old bird, the Major, Paul thought. He was a good judge of things. As the second half went on, the Cherries' number seven got more and more of the ball, and as he made his runs towards the near goal Paul had to obey the instructions he'd had and concentrate extra hard for that shot he had to get. At first the Londoners didn't seem to notice the shifting emphasis and they left their number three to cope with him, but more and more the harassed defender was beaten by the attacker on the run.

With more solo effort in the viewfinder the game began to make more sense to Paul, but it was as a cameraman rather than as a spectator that Paul was to get his biggest thrill from it. It happened near the end of the game when both sides were becoming frustrated with the thought of a goal-less draw, when all the planned moves and the obvious patterns of play were leading nowhere, and Paul could see, through the Major's eyes, that if anyone was to make an impact it was going to have to be the individualist.

Paul picked him up again as part of a wide shot, when he received the ball just inside the Whites' half. Then he gradually closed the lens in until he had the length of his body tight in the frame. Like a marksman Paul kept his finger steady on the button as the slight lean figure with the serious face hunched himself over the ball and began to run fast at the defence. He'd been snapping away without thinking, and with a sudden hollow feeling like spending too much money, he realized he'd probably only got one or two shots left – if that – and still no goals to show for it. He'd feel a real fool if the man scored after he'd run out.

As deaf as the player himself to the shrill shrieks of the Whites' supporters and the cries of both sides, Paul used both hands to hold the runner steady in the centre of the viewfinder. There were three men between the forward and the dockers' goalkeeper, and Paul could only hope that there would be a shot left, because this was surely the do-or-die attempt of the match. Still at speed, seven showed the first man the ball before slipping it past him to his left, then he pushed it between the legs of the second, and while the third ran backwards, keeping pace with him and holding off for the right moment to tackle, he glanced swiftly up. There was a Red running into space on the right, calling for the ball; there was a Red behind, screaming for the back heel; and there was a blur of red somewhere out to the left, putting three easy options open to him. No one could have blamed him for passing the ball as the Whites came racing back. But he didn't take an easy option. As Paul held him, clear and tight in the viewfinder, he went straight at the last White defender, the big number five, as if he intended crashing smack into him.

A loud groan went up from ten other Reds. He'd done the one stubborn, greedy, thing; he'd wasted a good run because he hadn't passed the ball in time. He had gone for one more man and tried to do the whole job himself, and he had failed. The defender's boot went into the ball with a dull thud and the big number five charged into him. Already, the other Red forwards were throwing their heads back in disgusted disappointment. It must have been the last chance. But the number seven had kept his leg well behind the ball, and as it was struck it bounced hard against him and spun sideways – and slightly forward – towards the goal. He had taken a chance, but with the knowledge that his own choice of action had given him the edge. Riding the charge, he regained his balance and before the number five could turn he was following the ball in towards the goal. Then, as the goalkeeper advanced, he picked his spot, and with a searing shot he cannoned the ball firmly into the net.

Great! Paul had clicked the button right at the moment of impact. And when he glanced down at the film counter he saw he'd done it on shot number twenty.

To thin cheers from the Cherry Tree Supporters, and high-pitched shouts of consolation from the Whites', the number seven was mobbed by the team.

Brilliant! A great piece of football! That was definitely the way to do it, Paul thought: skilful, not afraid to have a go on his own, probably cursed when he failed, but mobbed when he scored. A chance-taker; and, today, a match winner. No doubt. That was the way.

Paul gave a thumbs-up sign to the smiling Major below and stood and watched the last few minutes of the game from up on the changing room roof. And as he watched, like anyone does, coming out of the pictures and acting like the hero, Paul began to see himself in the same role. And why not? He could see it now. Forget falling over backwards to be one of the 'in' crowd. Stand on your own. Be your own man. Could he be like that? he wondered. Then, as he looked over the pitch from his solitary vantage point, the sun on his shoulders, he realized that he'd made a bit of a start already, over the sweets and the football trial. It was being so closely involved that he hadn't seen it before. But seeing someone else for a change enabled him, in some strange way, to see himself better. And he suddenly began to feel good.

Bolstered with that growing feeling of a new confidence in himself Paul handed the camera down and dropped to the ground. With some show he dusted his hands and his jeans.

'You looked as if you might have got the goal . . .' The Major checked the camera over.

'I did!' said Paul. 'Great! In a really tight close-up!'

'Oh, well done, Paul. Splendid.'

Paul watched the Major as he clipped the camera away in its case, taking his time over it, checking and re-checking the alignment of the metal inside. It was almost as if he were filling time, waiting for something to happen; and then suddenly, without thinking about it, Paul heard himself beginning to say some of the right words that had been eluding him all week.

'I'm ever so sorry about the other night. I should've come round, but these other kids wanted me to play football . . .'

It wasn't much of an apology; but it was a start, just the surface of what Paul felt inside about some of the things he'd done. If he *was* going to stand on his own, be like that bloke, then perhaps he could start by getting rid of the burden of self-deception he'd been humping around with him.

The Major seemed to understand, and he knew better than to leave a man standing knee-deep in awkward apology. He immediately helped him out.

'Water under the bridge, Paul. Forgotten and forgiven, old chap. But if you should feel like it, well now, why don't you come round this afternoon. Never mind my old stuff; but we'd be very pleased to see you for some tea ...'

'Oh, O.K.,' said Paul. 'Thanks.' And suddenly smiling he sauntered off to his Sunday dinner without a backward glance at anyone.

Chapter Fifteen

'PLEASE come in,' said the Major, when he opened the door that afternoon. He took Paul's denim top and hung it on a hook. 'Do make yourself comfortable,' and he led him into the living-room.

Immediately, Paul felt embarrassed at being fêted so, especially since he now felt so guilty about not turning up the other night. Now he could see it the way they must have seen it. He'd got over meeting the Major again, but he hadn't seen Arthur's mother since, nor Arthur today, and he felt distinctly uncertain about their welcome. Old men were notorious for being silly and sentimental about things, and the other two might be furious with the Major for asking Paul round. But the Major must have had more influence than most living-in grandads, perhaps he'd said something about him being helpful that morning, for before Paul could really feel uncomfortable perched on the edge of the big chair, they both came in smiling from the kitchen.

'Nice to see you again, Paul. Glad you could make it,' Arthur's mother said as she walked slowly across the room.

Paul stood up and searched for sarcasm with slightly narrowed eyes, but he could see none, and before he knew it he found himself responding to her sincere smile.

'Hello, Paul,' said Arthur. But his nose didn't wrinkle, and Paul knew he'd been forgiven.

He also sensed that he was being greatly honoured. Very rarely, he guessed, was the living-room table cleared of books and file paper, and very rarely did Arthur's small family sit up and eat a meal for its own sake.

The Major had found a clean cloth, and laid the table to Officers' Mess standards. He sat them all in their places, he gave them an apéritif of best natural orange (and two fingers of whisky for himself) and he carried in the ham salad as if it were a sucking-pig. And at the end, when the port would have been passed, he lit his pipe and like a good commanding officer he introduced the first topic of conversation.

'Now this Doran chap you were both asking about,' he said. 'Got any further with him, have you, Paul?' He turned in his chair to face Paul, who suddenly felt quite elated.

It felt fantastic to actually know something for certain. At last. Even though he didn't know quite where to start.

'Well,' he said, looking only at the Major, 'up here used to be an airfield. Before they built the houses and everything. There's a bit of the runway still there ...' He couldn't resist a quick look at Arthur; but Arthur just looked interested, not cocky any more. 'They had all different things going on – races and aeroplane tests and acrobatics ...'

'Aerobatics,' the Major corrected gently. 'Yes, go on ...'

'Well, and record-breaking attempts ...' He'd seen it all in the lady's newspaper clippings, but it was hard to sort it out now he had to tell it.

'But Doran. What about Doran?' Arthur prompted. 'He's what we need to know about.'

'Well,' Paul went on, glad to be steered, 'in the war it was all taken over by the R.A.F., a sort of reserve place for emergencies. First they had different squadrons of different things, Spitfires and that, and in the actual Battle of Britain there were Hurricanes here ...' He stole a glance round the table again as his confidence grew. Arthur was listening to him really seriously, and the Major, and Arthur's mother was puffing at a French cigarette with her chin in her hands. 'And a lot of people got killed.' Paul stopped again as the picture flashed through his mind of the bunker, and sitting on the edge of that field with Lorraine, and the pair of them feeling sorry together.

'Yes, go on. What about Doran?' Arthur was on the point of doing a nose wrinkle.

'Well, he was one of the men here,' Paul said quickly, 'ever so young, and a pilot, but not an officer. A sergeant. But he was one of the aces.' He said it with pride as if telling it linked him with the great man. 'A really good flyer. But one day while he was on a chase a dive-bomber came over here, and when the German saw all the planes were up in the air somewhere he dived down and hit the bunkers out on the edge, where the women airmen were, and more than twenty of them got killed . . .'

'WAAFs,' the Major put in, in a very quiet voice.

'Yes, that's right, and then it dropped some more and got the runway and some little cottages, and then it bombed Eastfleet and then it cleared off down the river towards Germany . . .'

There was a silence in the small room, letting in the sounds of nearby televisions, while the three of them waited for the climax to Paul's story.

'Well, then Doran came in for more fuel and bullets, but he couldn't land because of the runway. And on the radio they told him what had happened and said he had to go and land at Rochester. He'd got just about enough to get there. But instead of that,' he breathed in noisily before the last bit, 'instead he disobeyed the orders and he went off after the dive-bomber. And he caught him up over Sheerness, but he couldn't do anything when he'd got him because he hadn't got any bullets left . . .'

Paul knew the feeling. It had almost happened with the camera at the football.

'So he rammed it.' It was Arthur, in his quiet, certain, voice.

'Have you read it too?' Paul couldn't help asking.

'No, but it's the only logical thing, isn't it?' Arthur explained. 'If he'd let it go you wouldn't be telling us; so unless he threw snowballs at it he must have rammed it . . .'

The Major nodded his agreement.

'Well, that's right,' said Paul. What he'd give for a clever brain like Arthur's! 'He took a chance on the German gunner and he flew in over the top and pancaked his plane down on the dive-bomber's back . . .'

'Wow!' said Arthur. 'Then I suppose he crash-landed safely while the German plane nose-dived into the sea?'

'No!' Paul didn't know whether to be pleased or sorry that Arthur was wrong. 'He couldn't get his plane clear. They were locked together. And the crash had jammed his escape hood . . .'

'Then, what?' But they could all guess the answer already.

Paul said it as matter-of-factly as he could. 'They both crashed into the sea together; and everyone was killed.'

'Oh.' It was Arthur's mother. Then there was a long silence. 'And what's the moral of that story?' she asked them all. 'Apart from the futility of war?'

'None,' said the Major. 'No moral. Just the un-varnished facts.' He stood up stiffly and began to put some plates in piles. 'But we live in Doran House, and these chaps are doing a spot of research into the origin of its name . . .'

'Did he do right, do you think?' asked Arthur, the tact-ician. 'It was a one-for-one kill. He lost us a plane for one of theirs – and surely, numerically, British planes were more precious than the enemy's. We had fewer . . .'

'Yes, that's true.' The Major polished an unused plate

173

on his elbow. 'And if I were his C.O. – and if he'd baled out and lived – I'd have given him a jolly good rollicking for disobeying orders.' Arthur nodded, while Paul frowned. 'And then I'd have stood him a round of drinks in his mess for bravery!'

'Why?' Arthur's hands were on his hips. He wasn't going to lose a tactical argument easily. 'He'd lost a valuable machine for nothing more than an act of revenge . . .'

'Well, I see your point, Arthur. If that's all that counts.' The Major stopped working. 'But you're forgetting two things. One, he was a flier, a young man, almost straight from school I should imagine; and like the rest of us when we first enlisted, he would still be growing up, and like the rest of us, he was quite capable of doing one day what he wouldn't do the next. And secondly,' he went on, 'in something of this sort, morale counts for a deuce of a lot, too; and in doing what he did Doran probably boosted morale on this airfield and down in Eastfleet one hell of a lot, in ways that can't be measured. And don't forget the WAAFs: they played their part, first-class girls, I expect, and some of them had died, Paul said. By George, the girls must have needed a champion, someone loyal to them.'

'Yes,' said Arthur. 'All right, maybe . . .'

The Major bowed. 'Of course! I don't want to rub it in, Arthur, but the trouble with the war games you play with all your men lined up there in the other room, is that they take little account of unmeasurable things like emotion and morale. Perhaps your rules allow a few points here or an extra throw of the dice there; but there's no escaping the fact that they're just little lead figures without any minds of their own.'

'And they're only model *men* . . .'

Arthur and his grandfather, lost in their debate, looked round and remembered Paul.

'Well,' Paul said, very hesitantly, 'those model soldiers, they're *men*, aren't they? And those WAAFs who were killed, well, they were *women* . . . I know your battles are old-fashioned, Arthur, but . . .'

He came to a sudden halt. He didn't know how to explain his muddled feelings about the WAAFs, and the bunker they'd probably been killed in; but he knew that somehow Lorraine figured in all this; where she'd been with him, and what she was, and how he might feel if she'd been one of those WAAFs; somehow she had made him more aware of females generally – even of people like his mother, who'd been running herself into the ground in the shop but wouldn't give up; and of poor old Miss Simmonds . . . 'Well, it's a mixture, isn't it?' he finished lamely. 'It's not all men at all . . .'

'Hurray, Paul!' Mrs Little stood up and took a little bow. 'I must be getting middle-aged to need to feel appreciated. I can see someone here who'll make a very good and considerate husband . . .' But she had to rush on almost breathlessly to cover Paul's embarrassed look. 'Anyway, now, what about poor Miss Simmonds? She's having a rough time from all those he-men in the class, isn't she?' She looked at Arthur, willing him to come to her rescue in helping Paul get over her remark. 'Weren't you saying there was some special homework she wanted done, Arthur?' She stirred her coffee briskly and looked at her watch.

'Oh, it's nothing much. It's just this Doran thing again.' Arthur stood up to go, as if he didn't want anyone investigating his comments. 'She wanted us to find out about him, but he has,' he jerked his head at Paul, 'so that's more or less that.'

'Oh, I see. I thought it was something special from the way you spoke about it.'

'No . . .'

'But it is.' Paul felt better now, and he couldn't help butting in because he did think he understood what Miss Simmonds had been going on about.

Mrs Little had raised her eyebrows.

'Well, it's just that she wants to show people that we can find out for ourselves. That's all, really, except instead of just writing it down, she wants us to do it on a cassette or something, you know, make it more interesting . . .'

'Oh.' Mrs Little was standing up now and looking round for her glasses. Is that all? she seemed to say. 'Well, good luck to you both. I'm sure two bright sparks like you can come up with a good idea . . .' The Sunday interlude was over; and with a few mutterings about doing an essay plan by bed-time, she smiled at Paul and drifted into the kitchen.

There was a long silence in which nobody offered to make a start on the washing-up, and in which Paul had that uncomfortable feeling of having spoken his thoughts too readily, of having revealed the last secret . . .

Eventually the Major gave a little cough and Paul hoped they were about to be banished to the bedroom for a war game.

'And when has this commission of yours to be completed?' he asked.

'She didn't say. She wants to talk to us about it tomorrow; about the ideas we've got for doing it.'

'So you're not too rushed for time?'

'I don't know. Don't think so.'

'I think it's absolutely potty,' said Arthur. 'I could write it all up in a couple of lessons . . .'

'Oh, I dare say,' agreed the Major. 'That's true enough. And then your Miss Whatever-her-name-is would read it because it's her job to . . . and that would be that, eh?'

Both the boys looked at him, united in their lack of understanding.

'Well, don't you see, I could have sent the Regiment written accounts of all my stuff; as a matter of fact, I did; it's the best way for some things; but what do you do when you want to put your point across with a bit of impact? When you want to interest people enough to want to read about what's going on?'

Paul's eyes opened.

And so did Arthur's mouth. 'But we can't photograph something from the Battle of Britain which happened at two or three thousand feet! I haven't got a head for heights; and when I flap my arms I don't fly!'

Paul snorted, and the Major twinkled silently; but he left on his face one of those looks which told them that he knew of a way, and he was only waiting for them to discover it, too.

Paul thought about the camera; they were obviously being offered it to use, and his thoughts went naturally back to the changing-room roof; for a few moments he saw in his mind the patterns of play in the match below him; the super goal he'd shot, the Red number seven weaving in and out, the loner; and then, by contrast, he thought of Arthur's sarcastic picture of himself, flapping his arms to fly.

And then he had it! He knew how they could get Doran, the brave avenging flyer, on to slides.

'We run round,' he said, 'like aeroplanes, like in a game, sticking our arms out for wings; we sort of *stand for* aeroplanes, just two of us, one for the dive-bomber and one for Doran. And we take pictures. People'll understand that!'

With a very straight face the Major reamed his empty pipe. But his spirits had risen like wreaths of best sweet Virginia smoke. This was quite like old times in the Mess, leading on a bright protégé, making him use his brain and his imagination. He poured two more fingers of whisky, an act of self-congratulation for happening to get out the camera.

Arthur's face still seemed sceptical, but his words showed at least a willingness to think about it. 'We'd need some girls,' he said, 'for WAAFs.'

It was all Paul could do not to choke. 'I know some we could ask,' he said, studying his plate once more.

'Well, now,' said the Major, 'you chaps put that idea up to your teacher and see what she thinks about it . . .'

Arthur nodded. Paul said, 'O.K.' But before he got up Arthur had the grace to say, 'Oh, yes, thanks for finding out about Doran. How did you do it? Did someone tell you?'

'Oh, a lady helped me,' Paul replied. 'Just a bit of luck, really. But she didn't tell me. I read it all up.' And he was pleased to see Arthur and his grandfather absently nod their approval. To Paul, all of a sudden, it meant a great deal.

Chapter Sixteen

THERE was something about headteachers' rooms which never altered, however old you grew. Even when you were a teacher you were aware of an uncomfortable feeling of being out-ranked in them: and yet considering how hard some heads tried to put you at your ease it was hard to analyse why. It was probably the desk, Miss Simmonds decided. There would always be their side of it, and yours, and even when the head came round from behind it for an informal discussion in the easy chairs you knew the desk was still there – ready to divide you if the conversation took a nasty turn. Everything might be very friendly, but that desk-width, wherever you sat, was still there between you.

Otherwise, Miss Simmonds' thoughts were quite detached that afternoon. Having decided to resign she felt the calm of one who has nothing more to lose.

'Resign? Oh, come on! That's a bit drastic, isn't it? This problem's here to be solved, not to be given best. You may not have noticed, but I'm suppose to be here to help you, Brenda – and you've hardly given me a chance to do so yet ...'

He was smiling confidently as he leant forward in his low chair, sliding a few papers about on the coffee table with his finger-tips. But Brenda Simmonds wouldn't be drawn just yet. To her, he'd been more critical than helpful so far.

'Now, I'm not suggesting you should abandon the way you want to work. Heaven knows, I'm all for chasing any methods which help children to learn – and I'm sure you can get some good results. But the secret is to move slowly. Remember, I've not been here too long, and they're not used to having assignments and being left to organize themselves yet. It's something I've been working towards, but it must be done step by step. Drastic change can be fatal. So you must give them plenty of basic work – interesting, mind – and then introduce some of your, our, ideas gradually. Then, when the moment's right and you've got the class where you want them, select a good example of what you want, and show it to the others. Capture them by the evidence of successful work. That's the way to make changes . . .'

He smiled again and relit his small cigar. Still Miss Simmonds said nothing.

'But for goodness' sake don't say you're giving up after a week! I've got plenty of equipment and a good selection of useful books – and I'll really try to come in more myself. Now, at least you'll give me a chance to show that I can be helpful to you before you make a drastic decision like resigning, won't you? Do me a favour and give me a month?'

Miss Simmonds looked down at her hands. She was still far from happy about it all, but she supposed he couldn't have made her a fairer offer. Before giving in, though, there was still one thing she wanted to make clear. She spoke very softly.

'O.K. But Billy Richardson. What can I do about him? That's where most of the trouble starts . . .'

Mr Griffiths pursed his lips. 'Yes, I know; and don't think I'm unaware. If I had another fourth-year class I'd move him. I keep thinking I'm making a break-through with him; I try to give him responsibility – I've given him the football team to run for me, that sort of thing – but I don't really get anywhere. And I'd be lying if I said I knew the answer to coping with him. I've had his parents up – nice people, own their own business, and Billy gets everything he wants – but they're always busy, of course; and I suppose Billy just feels the need to rule the roost. Being big doesn't help him, either.' By chance he puffed a perfect smoke ring with his cigar, and they both watched it rise, expanding, until it got too large to retain its shape. They smiled at it, like children. 'To be honest, I just live in hopes that something might happen to relieve him of the continual responsibility of being the toughest boy in the school. Unlike a champion boxer, I suppose he feels he can't retire. No, I'm afraid he's just one of those problems we've got to battle with . . .'

Miss Simmonds nodded, feeling, strangely, a fraction happier in the head's lack of real help. At least the man wasn't pretending there was a pat answer to every problem and it was just she who was failing.

'Now, tell me more about your environmental studies. The new boy seemed very keen to get to grips with the estate.'

They were all new boys to Miss Simmonds, but she certainly remembered Paul telling her about the head's interest in the assignment; it had quite encouraged her at the time, since it was one of her own chosen demonstrations of the way she wanted to work.

'Oh, yes,' she said, brightening a little more, but with a lingering resignation still in her eyes. 'I had another chat with them today. They've found out who Doran was – you know, Doran House – and now they've come up with the idea of making a set of slides about it to go with their written work . . .'

'Really? That's marvellous. Well, you seem to have got them going. But how on earth are they going to show what happened in the Battle of Britain in a series of their own pictures? It all happened a bit way-up, didn't it?'

'They wouldn't say. They want the pictures to make their own impact. But I think they're in good hands. They said Arthur Little's grandfather knows about professional photography. He's advising them. And they spoke pretty knowledgeably about the light having to be good enough, that sort of thing . . .'

Mr Griffiths looked thoughtful. Someone with professional skills of that order might be quite useful to the school in time to come . . .

'Well, that's great. We'll just have to wait and see.' He stood up. 'And, look, we'll wait and see how things go in the classroom, eh? I'll come in tomorrow and try to be some help . . .'

'Yes, O.K.'

Miss Simmonds stood too. Was this the time when he went back behind his desk? There was an awkward silence while the final words were being formed. Eventually it was Mr Griffiths who said them. He turned to his desk and he took a small decorated tin from it.

'I don't know if this'll be useful in the classroom – for rubbers or sharpeners or something?' he said. 'My holiday cigars were in it; and they're all gone. It's back to normal now . . .'

Miss Simmonds smiled a small smile again and took it. 'Thanks very much,' she said.

The light in Victory Park was good. The September sun, like an ageing sportsman, was showing how strong it could be in shorter bursts, and Paul's only concern was the deep shadow it produced.

'Still, doesn't matter,' he told Arthur as they stood on top of the changing-room. 'The shadows'll make the pictures look better, sort of deeper, especially when we run round with our arms out. More like real aeroplanes . . .'

'Yes, very symbolic, as long as we're quick,' said

Arthur, who didn't want to wear the big swastika on his back for any longer than he had to.

'You two gonna be much longer?' Rita shouted up. 'I feel a right twit dressed in this lot on a Monday . . .' She took off her Guide beret and held it at her side. 'Don't you, Lorr?'

But Lorraine, strangely, didn't jump in with one of her perky remarks. She squinted up at Paul against the sun and just said, ' 'Spose so,' quietly.

'All right,' called Paul, 'well here's what we're going to do.' He stood firmly with his feet apart to give his directions, while Arthur made a noisy, corrugated descent from the roof. 'First of all, the WAAFs are crouching down there in the penalty area with their hands over their heads, sort of sheltering, and I'll be up here to take the first shot of them; then Arthur has to run in from the wing like a German aeroplane and he dive-bombs them. Then the WAAFs have to fall down dead — and you've got to lay very still, don't breathe, and Arthur has to run off . . .'

'Well, don't be too long, then,' said Rita. 'If I hold me breath too long I get the wind . . .'

'All right,' said Paul, sensing that giggles might spoil the scene. 'Listen. Then Arthur comes up here and does the shooting, and I come into the picture like Doran and I have to fly round the WAAFs and see what's happened. And then Lorraine comes up here and gets some shots of me chasing Arthur round, and I have to crash into him, and we both have to run round in circles with our arms getting lower and lower till we end up in a heap on the ground in this goal . . .'

'And then we all go 'ome and wait for a phone call from the telly!' said Rita.

'That's right,' Paul agreed, indulgently. 'O.K., we'll have a go then. We've practised with the camera, so if we're lucky we can get done tonight before the light goes down. Right! All get ready in position.'

Paul re-checked the camera, the loaded film, the lens setting for the opening shot. It felt good to be holding the thing in his hands again, possessively, professionally, just the way he'd been shown. The old man had been great – wouldn't even come to watch them – told them to get on with it and never mind being afraid to experiment. And Lorraine had been great, too. She'd pulled a face, and said she'd feel silly, but she'd agreed; and what Lorraine did Rita could be persuaded to do, too. And Arthur, well, Arthur was Arthur, but his mother had got round him. They could have done with a few more planes and airmen, and someone to help with the camera, but they'd not done badly – and here they were, ready to go, with Paul, director, first cameraman, and leading actor, ready to shout 'Action!'

Arthur, still not a hundred-per-cent certain, walked round and stood out of sight in the shadow of the changing-room, and the two girls crouched down where they'd been told. Paul, pleased with his sudden idea to use the football pitch to represent the aerial battle-ground, stood tall on the roof and focussed the camera on a middle-view shot of the two girls.

'Put your hats on,' he shouted. 'Proper uniform . . .'

With one or two inaudible remarks, Rita followed Lorraine in doing so.

'O.K. Ready? Action!'

Paul pressed the button and took the first shot of the sequence. It was a good, clear shot of the two girls. The whole secret, he had learned in that long and earnest lesson from the Major, was not to make the pictures too far apart, to take plenty to keep the story going. They could be clicked through quite quickly in a slide cartridge on the projector, and it would give a sense of movement.

184

Having set out to arouse curiosity with some opening shots of the two girls, Paul, very slowly, millimetre by millimetre, gradually closed in on them. He took them looking up and around them, looking frightened, their hands over their heads, then looking at one another with fear in their eyes. They did it very well, he thought. By the time these shots were married-up with some sound effects on a cassette recorder it'd be terrific. Still shooting, he closed-in tighter until just the two frightened faces filled the screen. It was great! 'Don't spoil it, don't speak, don't giggle!' he was muttering to himself. 'Hold it, hold it, hold it.' They were doing fantastically well; a second attempt could never be as good as this. Then, while the girls still held their scared expressions, Paul found himself moving in still closer, pushing the lens to the limit of its close-up range before it muzzed into a blur. And although he hadn't intended to do it, to differentiate between them, he found he had just Lorraine's head and shoulders in the frame.

She held her frightened look very well, looking at the sky, then at Rita, and widening her eyes. She was a very good actress. It was perfect. Then, suddenly, without warning, the mood seemed to break, she spun her head round and shot a glance up in the other direction. Her expression had changed. It had switched off, and she mouthed something.

'Clear off you!'

'Hey!' Paul lowered the camera and looked out at the real scene with his naked eye. It took a second for the iris to adjust; but there was no doubting what was going on. A boy was standing over Lorraine. Someone big, in a red track-suit. It was Billy Richardson.

'What're you lot doing on our pitch?' he shouted. 'I need this for my team in a minute. We've got a practice. It's all fixed up!'

'And we need it for what we're doing!' Lorraine retorted, still crouching, not sure whether she would spoil everything if she shifted her position and stood up.

'Rubbish!' Billy turned to face Paul up on the changing-room roof. 'This is a football pitch, Daines! For football! You play your stupid games anywhere. Go on, clear off! Before I 'ave to make you!' Then, to emphasize his point, he turned his back on Paul and with a belligerent move forward he suddenly pushed Lorraine hard on the shoulder to send her sprawling to the ground.

There was no knowing what Lorraine would have done had Paul not been so quick off the roof. She didn't get a chance to prove him right about the strength of women. He paused only to put the Major's camera safely in a corrugation. Then he was off the roof in a flash. He didn't know how he got down. He might even have jumped all the way. But without a second's hesitation, his feet thumping hard into the dry ground, he landed and started to run furiously at Billy.

The big boy turned to face him and squared up, his feet apart, his hands hanging limp by his sides, his fingers curling and uncurling in the football-terrace attitude of aggression. But Paul didn't care. Billy could have been ten hooligans, twenty, a hundred, all two metres tall. He didn't care what he had to take himself. Finally it was one against one, and there was going to be a duffing, a settling-up, and Paul was going to give it. This had been boiling up for days, and in a few seconds now it would be all over the ground! And there'd be a special thump for the dead bird! He ran at Billy with all the uncontrollable fury of lost temper, his fists flailing already, his feet ready to kick where it counted, and his head thrust forward like a battering ram, every part of him determined to smash into Billy and give him what he'd been asking for all week.

'Stop it!' shouted Lorraine. 'I'm all right!'

But Paul ran on. Nothing in the world could stop him now. He had a lot to settle, a lot to prove.

But when he got to within five blazing metres of the other boy he knew that he'd won, for, to his amazement, Billy suddenly dropped his fighting stance, and turned, and ran.

'Come here, you big coward! Come back here! Come here!'

But Billy wasn't hearing. Throwing hot, darting looks over his shoulder, he ran round the girls where Arthur was to have run, and back towards the near goal. His head was down and he was in full flight. It was no tactical run, this, no manoeuvring for a better place to fight. He was running away. He ran straight past the goal towards the changing-hut.

'Coward! Chicken!' Between angry gasps for breath Paul remembered their collision in that first playground game – when he and Billy had fallen hard together. Perhaps the big kid was remembering. He must be! He ran straight for the changing-hut, and before Paul could succeed in kicking out at his flying ankles, he'd got in through the unlocked door and crashed it shut in Paul's blood-red face.

'Come out, you great pilk! Come out or I'm bloody coming in!'

There was no reply; but from the close sound of heavy breathing Paul knew he was standing centimetres away with his back pressed to the rickety door.

'Come out!' Paul crashed the sole of his boot into the panelling. 'Come out and fight!' The red, white and blue R.A.F. circle pinned to his back stretched taut as he bent forward and rammed the door with his angry hands. 'Come out and fight! Come out and fight!'

There was no response, and Paul stood back to draw more breath. He was shaking with anger and frustrated

187

effort. And then he heard the voice. Once again it was Lorraine's.

'Leave it, Paul,' she said. 'I'm O.K., and he's given in ...'

Paul was gasping; but he felt cheated. Billy had been asking for this for a long time, and it would have given him great satisfaction to have let him have it.

'Come on, Paul; he won't be no more bother.'

Lorraine had put her hand on his arm; Arthur had appeared; and Rita had taken her beret off again. The sun went behind a hazy cloud.

'You don't have to descend to his level,' Arthur said.

Paul blew out, long and hard. Well, perhaps they were right. He let his hands hang limp by his sides and he took his time and blew, and blew. He began to see it a bit clearer, perhaps the way the others could. He could get in the hut and drag Billy out for a fight. Or he could walk off and leave him. In a way it was Doran all over again. Fight the enemy and go down with him. Or make the tactical decision to leave him to run off home. Except for one thing, one vital difference. Paul had managed to show his strength without losing anything himself. He hadn't given in, and he hadn't been put down.

So he left him. Like the Major had said, one day you did what the next day you wouldn't. And, perhaps the most surprised of all of them there, he found himself saying, 'All right, Richardson. Come out. I won't hit you. Just you say sorry to her, that's all.'

And after that he wasn't sure what he would remember most of that afternoon. The slow and cautious opening of the door, or Billy's muttered apology, or what followed on his own sudden decision to abandon the photography through the lack of light. Billy had barely covered the five or ten metres necessary before he could decently break into a run, when Paul had asked him, 'Hey! Tomorrow;

why don't you get all your men over to help us? We need some more, and they'll come for you.'

And Billy had turned round and said, 'Yeah, I might. O.K., if you like . . .' and he'd not broken into a run at all.

Paul gave Arthur the camera to take home till the next day. 'I won't be able to keep it safe up on my wardrobe,' he explained; 'not till later. I've got a bit of clearing out to do for my mum.' No one had understood, though; not even Lorraine. But she did begin to smile. And he felt very happy to settle for that.

Author's Note

THE war-time airfield, now built upon, which provided the background to this story is Gravesend Airport, in Kent. It grew from a field on which aviators could land by private arrangement to a proper airfield in the early nineteen-thirties. The airfield was known as London East and it incorporated a factory owned by the Percival Aircraft Company, who built the twice-winner of the King's Cup Air Race there (the Mew Gull which won in 1938 and 1955 and which was advertised as 'the fastest three-seater luxury aircraft', selling at £1,275!).

The airfield had a flying school and staged many popular air displays before the Second World War. On 4 May 1936 Amy Johnson left Gravesend in an attempt to break the England–South Africa record in her Percival Gull 6; but when the undercarriage was damaged she had to abandon the attempt and return to Gravesend. After repairs she took off again, and after 54 hours 37 minutes of actual flying time she beat the record for the 6,400 mile flight to Cape Town by 11 hours 9 minutes.

At the outbreak of the war Gravesend Airport was taken over by the Royal Air Force, becoming a satellite fighter station in the No. 11 Group. Various squadrons used the station during the war, and the airfield was frequently attacked. It was a convenient base for 'wounded' aircraft to use en route to their own stations, and it was heavily engaged in the Battle of Britain, flying Hurricanes. Towards the end of the war German flying bombs (V.1s) made Gravesend unsuitable as a fighter station (it lay in the flying bombs' path), and it was reduced to a care and maintenance base. In 1956 it was vacated by the R.A.F. and it was disposed of. It is now covered by attractive, settled, houses and is called the River-view Estate with streets named after famous Thames sailing barges. Nothing is left now of the airfield but local memory, the remains of an over-grown bunker, and a concrete strip which goes out into a farmer's field . . .

Although the characters in this story are fictitious, the idea for one of them, the flyer Doran, came from the exploits of Flight Sergeant 'Ginger' Lacey, a young and successful pilot who, among other things for which he is remembered, took off in bad weather one day to go after a lone Heinkel 111 which had just bombed Buckingham Palace. After shooting it down he found he could not find his way back to Gravesend in the bad weather, and he was forced to climb above the cloud and bale out. Like Doran, he became a local hero. But Lacey survived the war, and later, when he was posted to Germany, he met and became friendly with Erich Hohagen, the Luftwaffe ace.